RAGING JAKE

LEOGON PUBLISHING

STEPHEN DEGENARO

LEOGON ENTERTAINMENT
www.leogonentertainment.com
Melbourne, Victoria, AUSTRALIA.

First paperback edition February 2022
Published under the imprint, Leogon publishing
stephendegenaro@leogonentertainment.com

Book cover design by Youness

Printed in bound in Australia and the USA.
978-0-6453835-0-8 (Paperback)
978-0-6453835-1-5 (E-Book)
978-0-6453835-2-2 (Hardcover)

Table of Contents

Chapter 1

Hot lights and pain. Blood was on the ground, blended into the logo on the mat. Low slip potential, but it was a weapon. The eight walls of the cage rattled with the sound of the cheering crowd. They wanted more. More light, more pain. Two fighters were inside. Their coaches were about to leave. One voice went over every other.

"That's just dirt! You don't spit in a competitor's face!"

The announcer directed the crowd to the monitor up top. Last round ended early on a penalty. The black trunks got angry and spat in the white corner's face. A technical foul, but not a painful one. Not even to his pride. Callum, in the black trunks, bit his mouthguard hard in a snarl. He was in pain, inside and out. His right side was way worse than the left. His eye was nearly shut; cheek puffed out, and his jaw a little slack. He was breaking.

"Especially not this guy, Raging Jake!"

Jake, in the white trunks, was calm and collected. The spit on his face was long gone. He lacked any lasting anger over it. His mood was steady and calm. His face was stoic, sporting a single major mark just above his eye, the one good hit that he took all evening. The rest of his wounds weren't worth mentioning. The only pain he felt was from the lights. Their heat was worse than a bleeding wound.

The referee returned to the ring and waved them over. Callum kicked the ground and hopped over. Jake walked.

"Keep it clean," the ref yelled, finger at Callum. Callum wasn't listening. His eyes were wide and wild. The mouthguard was out. His gums were red. The next spit he let out would be flecked with blood. Jake stared him down. His rage was steady and level. It rose like a flashflood, not in a wave but an overwhelming presence.

"Fight!"

Callum moved before the word came out. It was a subtle snap-kick that looked faster than it was. Jake slid his right leg back in a partial retreat. Callum's hook-grab missed. He was going for a ground match, in the end, a technical victory. He lost the standing fight in the previous round and couldn't take another heavy beating.

Jake slid forward with his left leg and changed up. He was going southpaw again, left arm dominant, a switch-up from his previous matches and listings. He favored no side. He just swung and swung until something started bleeding. It was usually the other guy. Callum was on guard. He saw the swing and blocked his face.

Jake hit the neck. Callum wavered. His neck was sturdy, not bone-hard but still knocked against Jake's knuckles. Before he recovered, Jake followed through. His hand clipped off Callum's neck, and his forearm slid with a slicing motion across the flesh. It ended with his elbow pushing in. Callum was forced off balance. His hands were up, but Jake was down. Jake followed through again. Callum twisted with the blow and took Jake's shoulder to the arm.

Then, Jake attacked again. He stepped forward, right leg first in a deep lunge, and did the same three-tap tackle just under Callum's left-side ribs. Right in the soft gut. The knuckles hit hard ab, the elbow spiked against the weakened flesh, and the shoulder checked right into the viscera. His organs were under assault. And his core was destabilized—his feet went flat.

Jake stepped forward. His leg crossed between Callum's legs. He stood up with two flicker-jabs to Callum's face, both to his unworked left side. Callum didn't know where he was supposed to defend. They were inches from each other, but Jake still had the force of a baseball swing in each fist. His only way out of another pummelling, legally, was to retreat. He hopped back and was against the cage before he knew it.

Jake came forward, arms up, boxing style. Callum tried to kick, but Jake blunted it with a wide stance and intercepted it with his quad. No damage. It was like hitting an overfilled sandbag. Callum tried another hook grapple up top. Jake ducked back and reached forward. He switched in an instant and judo-swung Callum off his feet. The junior fighter kicked out in the air to try and get better grounding. He didn't want to end up on his back. He managed to land in a slide on his left shoulder, but Jake was already on top and pinned Callum's right arm between his thighs.

Then the ground game began. The audience cheered for the

end of the match. Jake threw fist after fist, from above his head down to Callum's, until the bruise turned into a broken ulcer and blood spat out from Callum's caved-in cheek. He was still kicking, so Jake loosened up. Callum's first move was to pry his arm out. Jake let him so he could grab it first.

"It's an arm bar on the ground!"

The announcer was just moments behind the action. Jake held Callum in a submission pose. His brick-like shins were flexed across Callum's chest and locked down his neck. He couldn't even watch what was happening from the ground. It was a shame Callum had such a long reach. That made it easier to break. Jake held the sweat-covered wrist in both hands, squished it against his chest, and heaved his back into an arch until all the resistance suddenly gave out toward his groin.

"My God!" The announcer was astonished. "Callum's arm is broke! Raging Jake has snapped at the elbow!"

The ref came in to pull Jake away. A broken limb was an instant loss, and Callum wasn't the man to contend against it. He screamed on the ground. Jake grabbed the ref's collar and pushed him over as he rose to his feet. Jake hopped up the side of the cage and climbed until his head was above the metal, closer to the lights.

What made the arena hot wasn't the lights or the fighting. It was the crowd. Their cheers turned to energy, like fire. It lit the whole place up. It was hottest for the one they cheered for, and they all cheered for Jake. He was the Rage of the Cage, the Animal Man. He thumped his chest to the beat of their cries: *Rage-In' Jake! Rage-In' Jake!*

"This will go down as one of the meanest, dirtiest fights in the history of mixed martial arts!"

The bell rang several times. Coaches and technical teams came into the arena. Jake lowered himself but not his mood. His arms and voice were both up. His ragged voice yelled along with the crowd. They drowned out the heaving moans of Callum as his arm was splinted and his body was put up on a stretcher.

Jake wasn't undamaged, but he was victorious. That beat out any hits and nicks he took. It was just like always. His team, his coach, his agent; he saw past them. As the world blurred, all he saw were his knuckles, bloodied by another man's flesh. He stayed in the ring until the crowd stopped chanting.

And then he heard the boos. He heard the fighting in the crowd, the disagreements. Callum's fans and supporters had never seen such a display. They hated him—and they hated Jake, too. No pity for the loser and no honor for the winner. It wasn't the dirtiest or meanest fight in Jake's career. It was just another one. Another day under hot lights and cold pain.

Chapter 2

D ark rooms and succulents. From the world of violence to the world of pleasure. Jake made his way to the penthouse room. The label was celebrating his victory before he even arrived. Sponsors bought drinks, made deals, shook hands, swapped spit—it was the more vile side of violence. The people who let him fight for a living were the kind that an honest man would want to throw down with.

Jake wasn't that kind of man. It was all necessary. He wasn't a brash youth clouded over with a heart of justice and a love and passion for the sport of fighting. He was 40. He was beaten down by Reality, the cruelest fighter of them all. He saw the world of dark lights and white powder lines as a blurry hallway that led him from one fight to the next, all to avoid the dark back doors where those hot lights couldn't shine. The realm of obscurity—once his body broke like Callum's, that would be his destination.

Until then, he was Raging Jake. Even when he drank until he smiled, that's who he was.

It was a big party for a small group. The penthouse held about 20 people at max. There were only about 15, but they all had a presence that filled the space up faster. The music was too loud to talk under, so people just shouted intimate secrets plied through loosened lips. A few stood around someone in the kitchen who was snorting lines.

A woman named Katie gave Jake a tumbler. "Special drink for you, darling," she taunted. Jake couldn't tell what was in it. The lights and sounds muted out his senses. It tasted like gin when he skulled it. He pulled Katie in for a kiss and tasted the cigarette on her breath.

He went outside, away from the lights and noise to the balcony. The lights and noise sort of chased him out there anyway. The windows still flashed with strobes, and the music thudded against the dull glass. He could feel the vibrations of people talking but could no longer hear what they talked about.

He took out his mobile and checked it. Still one message, and probably the same one. He held it up to his ear and tried hard to listen.

It was still Sara. ".... It's best to come back…Sort a few things out…." It ended earlier than he recalled. He checked why and the battery died. He stared at it, emotionless. His rage was sated, drunken, and held back, but it was there. It was always there about something. He only showed it when a punch could solve his problems.

He went back inside, where everything turned blurry and indistinguishable. The lights and the sounds combined. Jake thought the speakers were in the strobe lights, or the stereo in the corner was somehow producing tangible darkness where all the other lights came from to fill in.

Things got worse as he neared the group. Voices started to

attack him. He was blindsided by physical force. He remembered his fights and felt the punches that once rocked him from heel to toe against the hard 9th wall—the arena's floor. There was no ground in a proper fight. Two men floated and hit each other until one truly fell. The floor was simply a wall to push and pull against. Down was simply a state of mind.

Jake started to feel that sense of down. Every step felt like he was walking into a much deeper hole than he thought, and it startled him when his foot landed on the level. He stumbled through the room, not sure where to go. His wandering made the penthouse seem like a mansion—or a labyrinth. No hard walls blocked him, just walls of noise and color.

"Where you going, Jake?" Katie asked. He couldn't see her, and her voice felt like it was coming from inside of him. Like a thought he couldn't control. He said something but couldn't even hear what it was. Then he left.

The hall lights were a different kind of distractingly bright. It was all one color, which was somehow worse. There were no corners or edges to work around. It was all a uniform visual slush of repeating patterns, door after door. The floor pattern made him feel sick.

Jake wandered even further, not aware of where he truly was until he felt the warm buzz of the air outside. He was on the streets before he knew it and passed by all the late-night clubs and bars that were blurry concoctions of their own. He started sobering up just a little bit, and the voices that were once a mental screen became clearer.

A lot of people were angry outside. There were hot and

hateful words being thrown around. A few drunks meandered their way up to Jake, thinking they could find some sympathy for their problems with him, but he just shoved them away with their unfulfilled drink coupons.

Jake was no one's shoulder. He shoved them away back on their dizzying paths while he stuck to his. He wanted to get somewhere else, away from the distractions and blurring sensations. He wanted to find somewhere quiet, outside in the city streets. It was a completely greedy desire, and he was too drunk to fully understand that it was impossible.

The sounds became less dense, and he picked up on some of the after-party discussions and distractions that were going on. Men were cursing each other out, sometimes on friendly terms and sometimes not. No fights were breaking out, though. All the hot language sounded too shallow to commit to a real fight. Girls were battling off wolf whistles and generally raunchy things while being raunchy themselves just out of earshot.

Cars honked just because they could. They couldn't sober anybody up or get them out of the street. Anyone out driving was less responsible than the drunks who were hitting the legs back to whatever warm bench would accept them in the middle of the night.

Jake was a state removed from his usual TV-ready fare. He had a T-shirt and gym pants on, not the white trunks, and a sponsored robe. All of that was behind him in the penthouse. The silk robe was always heavier than it looked, and it was a loaner. He couldn't even get it dirty on the outside.

A young man headed directly into Jake and spun off of him.

Jake was too solid to knock over, but he was a wavering kind of solid. A boulder on loose gravel, not a tree. The young man took the stiffer end of the shouldering and turned back. He was aggressive. That one dodgy slam ruined his whole evening.

"What's your fucking problem!"

The tone sent Jake into a defensive stance. The guy came at Jake with his eyes wide and teeth clenched. A fist flew through the air, clear as day and amateurishly slow. Jake let it pass close until the guy was closer. The nearest thing Jake saw that reminded him of the cage was a lamp post.

He took the slurring drunk by the shoulders, swung him hard into the lamp, and stepped in with the speed and intent to plough straight through them both. He dipped his head down and butted the young man's skull with a crack.

They both went down, not to the 9th wall, but the ground.

Chapter 3

Dark and cold. Jake was barely awake. He didn't recognize where he was or what had happened. He was more dead to the world than when he was a dodging, staggering drunk. He was curled up on the floor of a one-man police holding cell with a stain of dry vomit in the corner, right next to an untouched wall-mounted commode. Mixed in with the sick was a bit of blood from the sore opening on the inside of his cheek.

The cell door opened. A police officer held the door. He looked like he had more important things to be doing that early in the morning. He waited until the cell's visitor walked in with a proud, intolerant stride. It was Brian, Jake's manager. A very slick man who was offset and disturbed by his prize fighter's accommodations.

He saw Jake on the floor huddled up in a fetal position, sound asleep and drooling. He was half-dressed from how he left the party the night before. His shirt was gone. All he had was his track pants and sneakers. Without his sponsorships on his trunks, he just looked like another dye-job bloke that was lucky not to be nursing an open wound in such a festering place.

"Up, Jake!" the officer barked. "You have a visitor!" He

jabbed his heel into Jake's shoulder. At any other moment, that would have been a fatal move and would have sent him walking with a disability leave. He got brave once he was sure Jake was still dead asleep. His body barely even rocked back. It was dead weight fastened to the hard ground.

Brian walked out on a mission and headed around the corner from the cells to a booking office. He immediately yanked the jug off of a water cooler and tipped it upward as fast as he could, spilling a little on the ground around the dispenser. He lugged it back to the cell where the cop was waiting. He looked surprised.

Brian passed right by and overturned the jug over Jake's body. Water gushed and glugged out. Jake woke up after the first few splashes, and his body scrambled as he was under attack. He lashed at the water and pushed himself up. He gasped against the steady stream as it poured onto his face.

The jug emptied. Brian tossed it away. The hollow plastic bottle bounced with a loud thud against the ground until it stopped in a roll. Jake was left, shaken and panting, in the opposite corner of the cell. Brian nodded to the cop and walked out. He expected Jake to heel-toe close behind.

They were out in a few minutes. The paperwork was thankfully brief and not too embarrassing. Jake watched it all go down. He was 40 but felt 14 as if his father came to shamefully release him from his past due consequences. It was business as usual for the background of the fighting world, though. The only thing shameful about it was that he didn't go to jail looking handsome for the night.

They left and boarded into Brian's car. It was a sporty

affair, a touring car that he could proudly show off to potential clients as a potential gainful benefit they would share if they fought for him. It was a carrot on the end of a long bloody stick. They drove in silence through the street until Brian reached a two-story house within the city limits. A dodgy little place with a For Rent sign on the lawn.

Jake got out and stretched as he circled the car. He leaned down through the passenger window as if he had the hubris to hold the car in place to keep Brian from driving off. Brian swept his hand through his hair, ignoring the thin part up top, and paid attention to his temples.

"My hair's turning grey with all the stress," he complained.

Jake held his head, but not to check his hair. It was as blond as he liked it, good for his image. The insides of his head needed cradling. "Thanks for bailing me out," he said. "I owe you one. Let's get back into training tomorrow—no rest for the wicked!"

"Jake," Brian said. Jake stood up, conversation over, and started for the house. Brian raised his voice sharply, "Jake!" Jake paused and went back down halfway through the window. Brian calmed his volume, but his tone remained resolute, "Jake, I'm gonna have to let you go."

Jake paused for a second—like his hangover slowed the words. "What?"

"I'm sorry," Brian said, suddenly apologetic but no less certain. "I'm through—gonna have to let you go...the money you owe me-"

"You'll get your money!" Jake said with the same unwavering resolution.

"When?" Brian shouted back. He put Jake on the backfoot suddenly. Brian never got that angry before. He was used to being disappointed or lecturing, never furious. He wasn't the rage behind Raging Jake, but he had his own font of anger to draw from. "Cause I ain't seen any plans or payments besides my own fee for the work I do for you. Which is diddly squat. I bust my guts to pick up the pieces while my personal life goes down the bloody drain!"

Jake looked away at the road to ease his mind from the cramped space of the car. "Listen," he began, "we're not done, ok. We're like Family, and we can sort this all out. All we need is one big fight that sets us both up, get us both out of the red."

"Jake," Brian started, "you're a great fighter."

"But?" Jake impatiently insisted.

Brian shook his head and mulled his thoughts into words. "There just isn't the coin out there for a fighter like you at the end of his career. And it's time I put my energy into the younger up comers. We had our time." Brian looked over. The subject matter weighed heavily on his brow. It was the one thing he couldn't lash back or talk past or fight against—age. "Hey? Look—it's a Sunday. I should spend some time with my Family. We will just have to ride off what you owe—just go our separate ways. I'm sorry. But I can't be putting you first and my Family last."

Brian rolled up the window while Jake stepped back. It was his turn to be disappointed, and he showed it until Brian was out of sight. He was staggered. He only got off the road because someone else rolled up and honked at him.

He intruded into the loft home and trudged over to the letterbox that was full of mail. Unwanted mail, everything overdue and disconnected and generalized, pointless junk. He let it all stay in and started down the overgrown walkway to the porch when a dog sidled up to him.

He bent down and petted the excited pup until its owner called it over with a sharp whistle. The dog abandoned Jake as easily as it befriended him and ran over to his grumpy old master. The man gave Jake a toothy snarl as he led the dog back inside. Jake realized his position—dropped off in an expensive-looking car, topless, mid-argument with an older man.

He went inside to forget the failed night and morning with the hopes that his day could be salvaged elsewhere....

Chapter 4

Lights were low, and the air was stagnant. Jake's partial home was little more than a den of past triumph and continued consumption. All the spirits and beer he drank in recent memory were preserved as litter on the floor. A definitive path was carved out of necessity where most of the trash didn't cross.

His main entertainment room was a bar unto itself. It had a bar, with plenty of storage for alcohol that was mostly empty, as well as a lounge of chairs, a side table, and a pool table that was missing a few balls. The walls were adorned with his career, pictures and posters, and clippings of his fights. He had trophies standing on specially made shelves that gathered dust and belts hung across half the wall, with enough hangers to compliment another wall-length that went unfilled.

Jake sat behind the bar and plugged his phone back in. There was a sideways whiskey bottle that still had a shot's worth in it. He threw it back quickly to nurse his hangover and went over to the nearest lazy boy chair to lounge the rest of his headache off. He shut his eyes and slept through part of the day. He awoke to the sound of his phone signalling a full charge not long after. And to his stomach twisting in pain.

Jake felt safe to drive. The lights didn't blind him, and only his guts hurt from all the heaving he didn't remember doing the night before. He picked himself and his phone up, threw on a less dirty shirt, and made his way outside to his garage. Brian had a gentleman's car for courting and touring business prospects. Jake had a black Mustang from one of his early deals that he kept and maintained with more pride than the trophy that he earned it with.

He went off to town and stopped at a cafe for all-day breakfast, just in time for lunch. He had a half-full plate of a hash consisting of eggs, cured beef, bacon, three kinds of peppers, and two kinds of cheese. He ate half of it and filled himself up the rest of the way on toast. A meal that size used to be just one of three throughout the day, but his stomach refused to take anymore. He didn't want to test it, either.

He got a fill-up on his coffee while gnawing away at the dry wheat cracker the place called toast. Once the waitress left, he undid the plastic to-go lid and took a flask from his hip. He added just a splash of his gin and then fixed the top back on. His phone buzzed. He got a message. He side-eyed the mobile briefly, unsure who it was. There were people he didn't want to talk to, plenty of them. Brian usually took those kinds of calls. Without him, they would all go straight for Jake.

It was MA. Jake contemplated it for a moment. He scooped up his phone, ignored the message, and put it next to his flask. He put cash on the table, grabbed his cup, and left his food half-eaten. He didn't have time to feel ashamed over it. There wouldn't be any meals like it in the future if he didn't get an agent.

Straight into town. The coffee gave him a stiff wake-up. His black Mustang powered directly into the mid-day traffic. He waited out the hefty, gas-hungry hums and growls of the engine until he finally got to the downtown row of rundown, nearly-gone businesses. He parked in front of Mighty Melvin's MMA studio.

It was a former yoga studio repurposed into a wide-space sparring and practice gym for mid-season fighters to work on as trainers and for up-and-coming youths to learn how bad they were in a sports fight. A rare few would go one to an amateur circuit or a few competitions, but most new members didn't last a month of getting rocked onto the floor of an eight-sided ring.

He wasn't there for any of them, though. Not for the rush bags or standing sandbags, or even the practice. He was convinced he didn't need it. The world would be, too. They only saw him win his fight. They didn't see what happened after. He made his way straight to the back into a closet of an office to meet with the owner, the Mighty Melvin himself. He was a few years older than Jake but was retired for an extra ten.

They set up and got straight into business, which resulted in a nearly instant air of silent disappointment punctuated by an odd thump against a kicking stand.

"Look, Jake," Melvin began, "have you tried Frankie a couple of blocks down the road?"

"Don't want Frankie," Jake said. "I want you to manage me."

Melvin shook his head. "Jake, I don't think you would fit

into our team, to be honest."

"All you got to do is arrange the match," Jake explained flippantly, "manage and collect -."

"Jake," Melvin said with his hand up, "nobody wants to fight you."

Jake rocked back in his seat, half proud and half perplexed. He wasn't sure if he was being insulted or not. "That's your job," he asserted. "To find somebody...not a bum, I need a money fight."

Melvin huffed a sigh as he moved a newspaper out from a pile on the side of his desk. The paper itself wasn't heavy, but the headline on it hit like a cement brick. It was the first look Jake had of his post-game stories. None of it was about the fight.

Police made the arrest on a city strip—after the fighter RAGING JAKE got into a street brawl.

It went on: *No charges have been pressed at this time. However, this is the third time in as many years for the now 'Aging Fighter.' He will appear in court later this year.*

Jake leaned back in his seat as the words overtook him. What was worse was the picture. They used his promo still from the fight before, but the on-scene photo showed Jake in his usual rage, shouting down at the officers that were arresting him—four men to hold back his arms as he roared up the sidewalk.

"I suggest you get help," Melvin said. "You know, counseling, that sort of thing?"

"Don't concern yourself with that," Jake said, smacking the paper.

Melvin shook his head again, Louder. "You're a liability, Jake. I can't manage you when you can't even manage yourself. Now please, if you don't mind, I've got work to do." Melvin went to it, arranging his desk and the papers all over it until Jake got up and left.

Jake had half a mind to storm out but kept himself calm and reserved. He ducked his head down to hide his face but couldn't hide his rage. It was rising in him; he could feel it. He was also surrounded by people throwing punches and denting sand bags. The nature of the fight got into him. He wanted to show the young punks how it was done.

They were good. He left before he felt impressed—or humbled. And before anyone noticed him.

Chapter 5

Jake slammed himself inside his car. It was hot and stagnant inside. The midday sun seared through the windshield, and the slick black exterior soaked up all the heat. He was in a hot box of pain as his rage started to well up. He pushed his hands against his face to try and hold it back. The pain just reminded him of a fight, which made him want to start swinging.

He lowered the seat and reclined back until he was halfway in the rear seats. He stared at the ceiling for a moment and calmed down. His rage never disappeared. It just simmered. It went from knee-deep to a puddle, just as inconvenient to splash around in.

He threw his mobile into the passenger seat and sat back up in a crunch. His abs hurt. It was a bad pain, a near strain just to sit up in his car. He looked around for a distraction. He had bottles of booze, some half-drunk, and sun-baked, occupying the center console. Some cans were on the floor, which made the whole car smell sick.

The whole environment felt like it was against him, a sore reminder of who he used to be and how he couldn't get it back. He grabbed the steering wheel and jostled it, knowing it would stay attached even against his rage. It almost didn't. He stopped once he heard the worrisome click of the wheel against its shaft.

Then he returned his attention to the phone. He remembered why he didn't want to look at it. There was a message he had to take care of. The phone rang right as he was considering it. He reached for a whiskey first, then checked to see who it was. Ma again. He picked the phone first but fisted the bottle neck just in case.

"Hey Ma," he answered. "Sorry I didn't call back earlier, I've been -."

"Jake, it's Sara speaking."

Jake winced at himself. He remembered her calling before and must have ignored her twice. But she was still calling from mum's number.

"Sara," Jake began, "tell Ma, I've been in recovery mode after my fight so -."

"Um, look, Jake," she interrupted, "about your mum -."

"Been nursing a few bruises," he began, trying to make the conversation about himself first.

"There's been an accident," she announced. "You need to come home."

She hung up. The message was delivered. Jake started piecing together what it could mean. It obviously wasn't anything good. He flooded his mouth with whiskey, choked it down, and made a break for the highway.

He rode out of town with his rage beside him. The Mustang

thundered across the tarmac past the hanging sign for Silver City Highway. 849 KM. It shook to the sound of the car's fury. There was nothing ahead of him but flat earth for the whole lonesome drive. And nothing was waiting for him at the end.

It took less time than he expected. He rolled into the old town he used to know. Silver City was not a city and was worth far less than any silver it may have mined. It was an unlikely place for a man like him to spring from. A man with renown and accolades and fame. Silver City had none of those.

Raging Jake should have been the pride of their tiny community, a man who survived long enough to escape it and see the world, but he was forgotten. He was as forgotten as the town was to him at the height of his career. Always an afterthought, a painful reminder.

That pain became far worse as he rolled into town. Everyone he met and saw seemed to know it was him by his car. It was the only one not made purely for function, the only gas-hungry highway car in a town full of pickups and trade-ins. He immediately stood out, but for the wrong reasons.

It made him angry.

Then, he finally arrived and settled in, and he was sad. His rage was submerged under a heavier current of negativity. It pushed him down into deep remorse. All he wanted was to free himself up again. He wanted to fight so the pain would go away.

Then came the funeral. Kelly Cambell, 1956 to 2014, dead at 59. Jake looked down on the grave, stuck in place, with a crumpled up bouquet in a plastic wrapper. The gathering was small and personal. Jake recognized the people who were there, but just barely.

One was his father, Richard, a man Jake had no love or hate for. He left for too long for Jake to feel anything other than his own constant, normal rage. Richard was 60, nearly as young as Kelly was. He was well dressed for a biker, but his neck tattoo was still visible.

Then there was Natasha, one of Jake's old friends he left behind who wore a police uniform, one of the more unexpected changes that ended up blindsiding him on his return. She grew into a natural beauty who wore her charming good looks like body armor. She was unrelated but still gave her honest sympathy to the gathering.

Richard stepped forward for a moment as Jake simmered over the grave. It seemed like he had something to say, but couldn't, so he retreated instead and went his own way with the rest of the group. They all headed back into town, to their homes or to the bar or wherever they wanted. The Cambells weren't the family that the whole town would celebrate in passing. It was a sad day, but for most of Silver City, it was just a weekday.

Natasha stayed behind for a moment and approached Jake more daringly. She put a hand on his shoulder, which made him shiver. He was wavering on alert.

"I must be heading back to the station," she said. "If you need anything, I'm here. Be nice to catch up before you take off." She took out a small card and tucked it into Jake's loaned suit pocket. "You can call me anytime if you need, okay?" She patted him on the back again and walked away.

Jake finally let go of the flowers. He placed them down at the base of the headstone. Looking at it felt like a punch he couldn't block. He just wanted his rage back. It was easier, straightforward. He couldn't punch the ground, though the thought crossed his mind.

He was distracted by the sound of a dirt bike engine kicking off and peeling out. It faded off into the distance of the town. He was left alone in the graveyard with his sinking thoughts and rage. He was home, and he felt out of place. He couldn't even go back to his new home because there were no more fights for him to take.

He was alone with his rage, in a familiar but still too different place in life. The one place that felt familiar enough to welcome him was the bar. He just hoped that hadn't changed much either. He wanted something familiar and easy to know. Something that he could settle with his rage.

Chapter 6

Silver City Police Station. A small precinct for a small city. Most of the cop cars were just personal vehicles with modifications and flashers behind the windscreen. A Commodore and a White Ute formed the at-station fleet in the morning. Their owners were inside.

It was a nice little place, a cozy office where occasional drunks and out-of-town brawlers would walk through overnight. There wasn't a need for hard criminals to take up space in the jail cells. Some who visited thought it was because all the hardened, criminal-looking men appeared to be the ones in uniform.

There were few less fitting officers in the force than Officer Harvey. He was a brutal-looking dude, even when doing mundane filings on the daily office grind. His hair was buzz cut down, and he had a soldierly posture. He was strong, so much so that his basic uniform couldn't hide it. He looked threatening even with a pen in his hand as he scribbled away at the document.

He sat in the center of a two-desk office. A few computers were on desks against the wall next to the filing cabinets in the corners. There was also a coffee table with mugs and a perpetually filled kettle that produced the same stagnant brew day in and day out.

Harvey wasn't alone in the office. Like all good officers, he worked with a partner, even on paper duty. Across from his desk was Charlie. He was a much more clean and presentable person, an officer of the people who were used to words and civility. He was in contrast to Harvey, who was easily recognizable as a cop who talked with his billy stick.

They both worked away as their silence held down the perp whose paperwork was using up all their time. His name was Gavin. He had long, greasy hair and a lithe, lanky build. His head constantly bobbed as he worked as if he was quietly laughing at a joke in the back of his mind.

The clock ticked away for them as they passed their time with the boring backend of their duties. "Six," Harvey listed off. "It was nighttime. Seven. The car was traveling about one hundred and thirty kilometers. Eight—good. Nine—good. Ok. Ten, I believe that the contents of this statement are true and correct." He tapped his pen with finality as he punctuated the last sentence.

"I hate admin," he said. "Don't we, Charlie?"

"Yeah," Charlie nodded. "Hate it."

"We all on the same page?" he asked, pointing between Charlie and Gavin. Gavin reeled his head up, half nodding with a dumb grin. Charlie nodded normally. "Good then," Harvey said. "Best we start getting traps before our Rabbit goes underground." He put his pen on top of the form and slid it across his desk to Gavin. Gavin signed it with a shaky hand and passed it back. Harvey stored it in a vanilla folder and locked it down in the bottom drawer of his desk.

"Charlie," Harvey ordered, "walk him out. And make sure you plaster the town with posters."

"Sure thing," Charlie said. Harvey clipped a set of keys onto his belt while Charlie escorted the energetic Gavin out of the station. Harvey waited for them to leave sight before he ducked back down and undid the lock on one of his drawers. Inside was a shallow vase.

He held it up to his nose and sniffed hard from the rim. Whatever was in it put him in a heightened state, and he placed it back carefully to recover. He sniffed again while he was down and out of sight, then sat back up and looked around. All clear. All alone.

He laid back in his chair and observed his surroundings with a proud eye. It was all his. All the power and prestige he could handle was in his control. He looked over at a framed photo on his desk. It was an old one, but meaningful. He and Natasha stood side by side, out of uniform and warmly embracing. It was a time that had passed, but one worth remembering with each ticking second that went by.

He had a pride inside him that was always there, cocksure confidence that his actions would always benefit him. He lived his life in that moderate-high, sometimes bumping it up even higher, and was never without his sense of pride.

Chapter 7

S ilver City was hot and dry. The heat led people to boredom, the doldrums of facing a surrounding horizon of nothing but dusty terrain of the Australian wilds. The dryness led people to drink. As with any small town, the most popular and well-respected establishment was the pub. The Salt Lake Pub, specifically, named after the crystalized flats outside the town of the prehistoric lake that no human ever saw filled with water.

There were three cars parked out front, marking it as a very slow morning for the pub. The sadness of the recent passing must have gotten to some, but most just stayed away. There was a Harley Davidson motorcycle, years old and past its prime but maintained and cared for extremely well.

A few people filed out of the front, past the big black dog named Max. He had his own sign above where he sat. He was part-time mascot and part-time bouncer, always the first to get excited over fights and the last one anyone wanted to finish them. He barked at strangers as they passed and stared longingly at the regulars who he knew would give him their spare food if they had any.

One man entered against the flow. It was Richard, back to his usual gear and colours. Whatever gang he was part of was long since defunct, but he carried on their spirit as a proud member regardless. He wore a rag over his head, a butchered and twisted Union Jack. He took a slow drag of a cigarette and blew it up in the air. The smoke combined with the dry dust and tumbled out of sight in the crosswind of a passing car.

Richard walked up to Max. Max sat down obediently and received a hand on his head. Richard liked the dog. They were both scrappy and ornery on the outside but loveable to the right people. He just hoped the right people were nearby.

He stubbed his cigarette against the blackened doorframe and tossed it before he even crossed through the saloon doors. The pub was cozy, a small place for familiar drinkers to hang out, and was decorated with personalized local flavor. He looked around at the people. A lot of them came from the funeral and were whittling down their sadness one sip at a time.

Richard picked out a stool by the bar and saddled up to it. He caught sight of a hanging picture on the wall of three familiar folks, many years younger. Jake, AJ, and Kelly stood together, smiling, like a family without a father. He couldn't even see a place where he could have belonged in it.

"Drink?" Sara asked. She snuck up on him, but he didn't jump. He got tugged out of a warm-hearted delusion to the cold, dry ground.

He opened his mouth and let the answer hang for a moment. "Water, no ice, thanks," he quickly rattled. Sara nodded and brought it back just as he pulled out a plastic case full of pills. He put one in his rough palm and threw it into his throat just as the glass landed on the counter in front of him. He chugged half the water in one breath and sighed with relief.

The frame caught his eye again. It wasn't the biggest picture on the wall, not the most noteworthy, but he couldn't stop looking at it. He stood up and held his glass high until he could tell that he had someone's attention.

"To Kelly," he declared. The guests all caught on and cheered "To Kelly!" with him. Richard scanned the crowd and saw them, eye to eye, one by one. There was a lot of sadness but also a lot of gratefulness. People missed her, some more than him. While he had the room's attention, he decided to speak to break the silence.

"I'd like to say a few words, if I may."

He couldn't. The doors flew open with a bang. Someone attacked them. A huge man, bigger than most, stood in the doorway, and his posse blocked it as they swarmed in. Richard could tell what a gang was on sight. He judged their appearance by the reaction of the rest of the crowd. No one was happy to see them.

The man at the lead stood tall and wide. He wore a bandana over his nose and mouth like an old western bandito. He strode with a purposeful length to each gait as if he was silently bragging over how much ground he could cover in one step.

He had colours, too. All his crew did. Black shirts with red Stars of David. Something told Richard they weren't a religious group. Half of the crew looked Asian, maybe Polynesian. The rest looked like locals. They had the same bandanas and shirts.

What threw Richard for a loop was he heard no rumble or

roar of motorcycles arriving out front. If they were bikers, their rides were somewhere else. Which meant they were familiar enough with the town not to need them.

The huge, leading man reached over and stole a pint from some poor bloke that was in his way. He passed it down the counter to his second man, who passed it on to the next one after as the whole gang crowded up to the bar.

"Looks like we missed happy hour!" he shouted. His crew laughed and made a ruckus while everyone else sat further back in their booths and chairs to avoid them. No one was getting up to leave, though. The way out was still blocked by pestering bodies.

The gang turned to Sara across the bar at last. They overwhelmed her with their presence. A heavy scent of exhaust and oil filled the bar, even over the smell of hops and wheat germ. Sara glared the man down with the whole bar separating them. Richard clutched his water tight and prepared to finish it while he made his own careful observation.

It was suddenly hot in the Salt Lake pub, with a different kind of heat than the sun. There was a rage there, faint and bubbling just under the surface, hidden behind the smiles that were hidden by bandanas.

Chapter 8

Silver City Hardware store, an old mom-and-pop shop run by the most recent and well-established pop of the family: Joe. Joe was old and sun-beaten. He had a leathery face of deep, disappointed wrinkles and smoker's lines. He dressed like someone who would bum around outside, yet he owned the place, and no one seemed to mind. It was his place to own as he saw fit.

The stock was pretty basic fare for a rural town. It ensured that everyone, even those passing by, would have access to a tool kit of wrenches, screwdrivers, pliers, and all kinds of nuts and bolts to fix just about anything. But it was small, not a warehouse. All the larger equipment was in the back and was represented by old hand-written signs taped up along a back wall with a couple of pictures of what was on sale out of the garage.

Jake was wandering around, lost and a little confused. He was killing time until he decided on where he should go next. Silver City didn't seem like the place for him. There was one less person that would have wanted him there and one more that he didn't want to see at all. Seeing his dad at the funeral reminded him of his rage but didn't add to it.

That rage was always there. It was always because of him, at least at the start.

Jake eventually wandered up to the front and got his essentials. A pack of cigarettes and a book of matches. Joe's hardware even had tools for fixing personal problems—and making them.

"She was a lively one, your mum," Joe said as he clicked in the prices, manually and by memory. "Often, she'd make the two-hour trek into town on foot. A lot of up and go to be walking here—Two, sometimes three times a week."

Jake listened silently. Hearing about his mom just made him unsettled. Especially fond memories people had. He couldn't be angry that they missed her more than he did.

Another customer came in. The sound of the bells over the door gave Jake a start as he turned around. What he saw gave him an extra bump in his chest. An officer in a clean suit walked in with a clutch of papers in his hands. He plopped them onto the counter to alert Joe's attention.

Jake checked them over and suffered a third arhythmic stroke of surprise.

"Joe," Charlie said, "I'll leave this with you. Can you see it's placed on your front window?"

"Righto," Joe said. He peeled the top poster off and slid off his seat to tape it up to the front, next to other kindly offered community flyers.

"Right," Charlie said. He nodded to Joe and Jake courteously. "Good. You blokes have a good day." He nodded his head and tipped his invisible hat as he walked out. Jake started walking after him, threateningly. Charlie was out of the store before he noticed. Jake checked the sign again just before Joe hung it up, then exited to look at it through the dusty glass.

He knew that person. *Wanted for Vehicle Manslaughter. If you have any information on the individual's whereabouts, please contact the police.*

Jake knew he had to find that person before anyone else, even though he was a stranger and had no clear idea where he could be. It was the only other person he was connected to in town. Same dimpled cheeks as their mum. His brother AJ.

Jake's insides welled up with rage and confusion. He felt heat in the light and ran for the first shade he saw: The pub.

Chapter 9

The Salt Lake Pub was loud and dark. It was full of taunting, raucous voices of the gang of black-and-red shirts that took it over. The mourning patrons left, as they could, or stubbornly stayed only to be outnumbered and underclass by the surprise visit from the gang.

The crowd was havocing the pool table off in the corner. They intruded on a game and broke it up. Some of the members were failing to juggle the balls. One picked up the 8-ball and dunked it into a corner pocket, mockingly taunting the actual player for losing, utterly disregarding the rules. And his friends all laughed about it.

Richard and Sara were at one end of the bar while the rest of the gang centered around their large patriarch at the other. The masked man leered at Richard with a knowing look. Richard could tell he was being recognized and slowly started to realize who it might be.

"Don't stare," Richard whispered to Sara. She went down the bar on her own business towards the phone. She kept her eye on the leader while she prowled to the employees-only corner, but she neglected to anticipate the true lawlessness of the gang. One of the members hopped over the bar behind her quietly and yanked out the wall-mounted phone cord just as she reached for it.

Richard stood up just in time for the tall gang leader to scoop him away with an arm across the shoulders. Richard finally realized who it must have been. He was in disbelief, then disappointment, and was leading into a disgusted revelation. The man around his shoulder was an old rider of their colours. A young man named Tony, now roughly 40 but still in the prime of his wasted life.

"Fell off the face of the earth, Stranger?" Tony asked jovially. "How's retirement?" He shook Richard a little bit.

"We just had a funeral," Richard admitted.

"My condolences to you all," Tony said sarcastically. "I remember your ex-missus. Always tragic, losing a loved one."

The crowd of gangsters suddenly shrieked as a man came out of the restroom. He'd been in there since before they all arrived and was shocked and confused by their energy. He was an older man, a roughneck worker, who took their hoots and hollers with a timid wave and wandered back over to the pool table.

"My," Tony sighed, "how things have changed, huh?"

The mockery continued in the pool corner. The man from the restroom was held back while another young, lithe gangster held the pool cue out of reach. He whipped it around like a baton and faked passing it back only for the older man to clutch at the air. Then the ragged youth snapped the stick over his knee and twirled both ends while his mates laughed it off. He handed it back to the old man, who was still too confused to get irritated.

"Not too good with English," Tony mentioned, nodding over to the crowd. He held his hand up high, palm flat toward the ceiling. The gang members fell quiet. They turned one by one, signaling to each other to pay attention, and the whole pub was suddenly quiet. "That's where I come in."

Tony dropped his hand down sharply to his side. In an instant, the gang turned feral. They went from being juvenile pests to real dangers. They yanked away tables, threw chairs, and tore everything off the walls they could get their hands on. Richard was stunned.

"Hold me beer," Tony said, offering Richard a pint glass. He also bumped a cigarette out of a carton in Richard's direction. Richard shook his head. Tony shrugged and lowered his mask, revealing his true thick-jawed face that was so much harder to miss than his eyes.

"Now," Tony began as he lit his cigarette up, "I'm sure you can understand our situation here." He puffed up the light at the end and dragged a thin stream of smoke. He was smooth despite appearances and despite the chaos that he commanded in the background. "We can't have a club member willy nilly dip his fucking fingers into the cookie jar... I mean, back in the day, you would never have done that?"

Richard tensed up as he reckoned Tony's words. They went deep and stung him in an unguarded place.

"You see your son," Tony instructed, "be a good father, send him my way. It ain't his money. It ain't mine. It won't be my head on the chopping block, I can assure you. I'm just the messenger." Tony laid it all out with a very certain, unspoken threat directed at Richard's head. "You be the brains of the family," he said sweetly. "It's just business."

Tony flicked a card out of his dark jean jacket and shoved it under Richard's head bandana. Richard stood firm and took the disgrace while the chaos continued. Tony nabbed the beer from Richard's hand, drank it down in one smooth chug, then handed it back to Richard. His mouth was wet enough to give a piercing, factory-siren whistle that stopped the havoc within a second. Gangsters with objects held over their heads slowly lowered them as if they had been caught.

Tony waved his hands with an "Alright!" shout, and the boys all followed him out. The ones that spoke English threw out an insult or slur as they passed. The ones who didn't did the same in a mixture of their own languages, reveling in their own private jabs at the locals.

Eventually, no one was left but the scared patrons, the incensed bartender, and the static, stoic Richard. They all held fast as they listened to the sounds of raucous cheering fade down the street only to be replaced by a cacophony of bike motors that shook the air like a quake. It was loud outside and desperately quiet inside.

Chapter 10

Jake's Mustang was hot. Every part of it was hot to the touch. The leather work on the wheel made it hard to grip without a sting of pain going through his palms. All the fighting in his career couldn't ward that kind of pain off. He was used to a different kind of heat in the ring. He was about ready to thunder off to the pub when he heard the sound of thunder overhead. It couldn't be clouds.

He saw bikers go past. Three took up the whole road, then a staggered and chaotic horde of them followed. They had no regard for the law and weren't being stopped by anyone at that moment. He waited them out as they whipped past, down the road behind him to some other town or the outskirts where no one would chase them.

They were coming from the direction of the pub. There were plenty of other places in the middle of town, but they weren't the kind of places a bike gang would hang out. His stomach dropped as his rage grew. He only had one place to go and one thing to do, and he might have already missed his chance. Once the last of the bikes were gone, he tore out in his own way and hurried to the pub.

As soon as Jake pulled in, Richard rolled out on his Harley, purely by coincidence. He rode off in a different direction than the bikers had. Jake got out just in time to watch his distant father vanish even further away. They hadn't exchanged a single word all day, and Jake worried that they never would again.

The worry made him angrier.

Seeing the state of the pub made him furious. His fists clenched as the saloon doors swung open. He saw the state of wreckage like a hurricane wind blew through. Tables and chairs were tilted over. The cash register was busted apart, the pool cues were snapped in half and scattered on top of the table, puddles of undrunk beer were splattered across the floor. The audience present hated it. The fearful and irritated patrons all took to one corner together while Sara surveyed the damage. She was the first one to tilt her head up and notice Jake's arrival. Everyone else noticed him when he hollered.

"What the fuck happened?"

Jake made his way toward the bar and fixed a chair on his way past. His foot fell heavy on a picture frame, and the glass crunched against the floor. He picked it up and saw his younger self, his brother AJ, and their mum. He held the corner of the photo in a pincer grip—the kind that could cut off an aortic vein if it got a solid reach past the neck muscles. A killing grip.

"Don't touch anything," Sara warned. "I've called the cops."

"Dirty fucking dogs," one of the old men against the bar said.

Jake heard a ringing. First in his ears—like a shrill rush of water. It was blood filling his face. Rage was evident. The muscles in his face were worked out into a twisted complexion. Then he heard a more rhythmic ring that silenced itself in his pocket. His mobile went off, then went silent again, and he was the last to hear it.

He was the first to hear a car door slam out front. He turned with a guarded start to the entrance as Harvey came in with Natasha close behind. Everyone was on edge and thought it was some gangster coming back to finish off some unbroken piece of furniture they didn't see. It was almost as bad.

Harvey made a wide berth with his legs as he walked. He took up as much space as possible and moved in an unbroken, constant gait that pushed everything and everyone away from him. He gave no compromise or space for others. Natasha followed behind with a camera and took pictures of every unique angle of significant destruction she could while still staying on Harvey's heels.

"Morning all," Harvey announced as he casually waded through the middle of the carnage. He turned to the bar where the impatient owner waited with her arms crossed. "Howdy, Sara," he said. He took out a notepad and pen from his shirt pocket and clicked the top to get started. "What a mess," he summarized.

Jake, meanwhile, made his way to the only other place besides the entryway that was free of debris and evidence, which was behind the bar with Sara. Natasha glanced at him momentarily, then went back to her job with her boss. Harvey made notes of what he observed. He turned to a group sitting on a messed-up table and jotted it down like he was filling a report out on a zoo enclosure.

Then Jake's phone rang again. It interrupted the silence enough that the cops got distracted. Jake looked down at it, then up at Harvey, as if he was intruding. Harvey smirked and pointed his pen down at Jake's pocket with a nod. No rules against talking while the police were present, so long as it wasn't incriminating.

"Hello?" Jake answered.

"Jake." It was his brother. "Jake, it's me, AJ. Listen -."

Jake hung up the call and side-eyed Harvey. The officer approached the bar and made sure that, as straight as the approach was, he gave Jake nothing but his shoulder. He turned to face the rest of the bar like a sheriff in a saloon. "We'll do our best to find the ones responsible for all this. Everybody stay put while we get some details."

Jake immediately disobeyed and tried to leave. He got halted by Harvey's arm. It was stiff and well-balanced, a solid arm bar. With more force behind it, the cop could have delivered a solid connecting blow that would have slid up Jake's chest and clipped him in the throat. But he didn't. He just held it out like a toll road blocker and waited for Jake to give him some of his attention.

"Your name, buddy?" he asked.

Jake paused to determine if he could trust something as personal as his name with a stranger like Harvey. He saw into the man of law's wild eyes and decided not, but he did regardless to uphold the peace of law. "Jake Cambell."

Harvey immediately tilted his head in a sympathetic gesture. "Sorry to hear about your mother," he said. He glanced behind him to Sara. "My condolences. Never a pleasant part of the job, that I can assure you. It's tragic. We are doing our best to locate your brother. A terrible accident." Jake tried to walk away without getting bothered. "Has he tried getting in contact with you by any chance?" Jake paused on his way, then shook his head. Harvey continued as if Jake told him far more than he meant to. "You know where he would go?" Jake shrugged.

Harvey nodded his head and gave an audible, confident whisper of a chuckle. "Well, the local hospitals have been put on alert. He could be suffering horrific injuries from the crash. For all we know, he could be dead in a ditch someplace." He stifled his smirk and turned to Sara across the bar. "You say club members did this?"

"Bastards' faces were covered up," an old man across the floor said.

"I see," Harvey quickly assessed. "Possibly a rival gang passing by." He turned to Jake, halfway to the door, and locked him in place with a sudden analytical glance. "A territorial thing. It happens."

Then Jake got another call. He answered it quickly without checking who it was.

"Jake speaking," he answered quietly.

"Jake, it's AJ," the voice said. Jake kept his eyes locked to the side, in the direction of his phone. Harvey was locked onto him as if he was trying to listen in with just his eyes across the room. He wasn't investigating or making any more notes. He just watched Jake.

"Call back later today," Jake calmly announced. Like he was talking to an agent or a brand, just an inconvenient but formal tone of voice. Jake pocketed the phone and turned without checking Harvey's expression. The cop was dissatisfied.

"Okay," Harvey said with a clap of his hands. "Let's start noting a few things, shall we?" The two walked away from each other. Jake exited the bar to find somewhere else to talk, and Harvey troubled the floor to keep a record of the chaos that he missed...

Chapter 11

U p the road from Silver City were an old abandoned weighing station and truck stop. There were no trucks parked, only motorcycles and a few disheveled vans. The place looked like a building that was bombed out or barely survived a fire in the past. The windows were all boarded up, and the doors were reinforced with corrugated metal sheets.

Inside was a clubhouse, a hoarding place for treasure and plunder of the modern-day dusty bandits. Tony's gang used it as their hideout and clubhouse, an off-the-books official place where they could gather up and relax after a solid day of rampaging. It was out of range of police patrols and under their local radar.

The members used every part of the station for their ends. The interior of the former convenience store was converted into a lounge, with plenty of stolen couches and recycled fodder from dumpsters. They had a fridge full of beer and shelves full of stolen bagged and canned goods.

Most of the bikers lazed around and chattered with one another. The groups were split by their respective languages. The English speakers held the most sway and took turns first on the couches, feet up and dirt everywhere. Meanwhile, the

Polynesian and Filipino guys worked in the garage. Some worked on repairing the petrol tanks of the bikes. Others took up an isolated corner to work on bricking packages of thick, white powder.

Tony oversaw the room from his position where the clerk's counter was. It was his desk and office table, with scattered newspapers and other documents that were weighed down by empty bottles and stained with dirt and oil. He hiked his feet up from his chair and held a quorum over the scattered gangsters. Those who bothered listening to him held higher positions than those on break or worked out of sight.

"My bet," Tony said, "Richard's protecting him."

"Possibly," one of the men agreed.

"Problem is," Tony continued, "we don't know where he lives."

"I don't think we gonna catch him," the gangster replied. "Long gone, sitting on some fucking island whilst we on a wild goose chase. Say it's too late."

Tony started to shake his head to respond but was interrupted by the chirp of his phone. He pulled out his mobile and snapped it to his face in a quick, smooth motion. On the other end was a gruff, confident and sinister voice. The caller ID was listed as "Pig."

"I need you to keep an eye out around the pub," Harvey said. "His Brothers is in Town."

"Righto," Tony agreed. "The old man was there early too, Richard. Get address details?"

"No," Harvey replied. "He left the scene before we got here. Nobody here knows his locale here. The Brother, Jake? Longer he stays, the better. We have less than a day to shake this tree to see what fruit bears. Got to go."

With that, the connection severed. Harvey's phone, which listed 'Aunt Ethel' as his contact, went dark, and he slipped it back into his pocket. Gavin was in the corner of his office drinking a beer. Tony clapped his hands and rubbed them together excitedly. "Ok! Looks like the Brothers in Town for a while."

"That would be Jake," Gavin said, "am I right?" He hunched over with a devious grimace.

"Yeah," Tony said. "You know 'em?"

"Oh yeah," Gavin said. He strolled over with a swaggering gait to Tony's desk. He brought his pinky fingers together, palm still gripping his bottle tight, and hooked them together. "We like that." His sly grin and dirty laugh were more informative than Tony asked for.

Later on, Harvey returned to the pub and checked the exterior on a passing-by patrol. He waited by his car with a cigarette while Natasha finished up her on-scene interviews with everyone. He watched her through the window as she talked to Jake. His eyes smoldered like the grass-killing sun. He saw Natasha talking with her notebook down.

When she finally finished, she exited and saw him waiting with a bit of surprise. She was within walking distance of the station already, but Harvey seemed to insist on picking her up. He got in the driver's seat and waited for her to enter on the passenger's side.

"You know him?" he asked.

Natasha gave him a quick look. "Jake and I dated," she answered. "School days."

Harvey drew even harder on his cigarette in a long, controlled drag. He let it stir around in his throat a bit before he blew. "The boy's got an attitude problem, don't you think?" He exhaled and filled the top of the car with smoke.

"He just lost his Mother," she said. She waved her hand over her face and turned the air vents up and away from her. "Can you not smoke when I'm in the car?"

Harvey smirked and lowered his window. He flicked the cigarette out into the street. It skittered around until it stopped just shy of an old gutter.

Chapter 12

The next day, Jake got up early and headed to the local real estate office. He had some family matters to attend to that couldn't wait or be delayed. He had to plan for some visitors and figure out what his exit plan was. He was still a destitute former fighter. There was no career waiting for him outside of Silver City, and none waiting for him in it. He felt hot and bothered, anxious. The pain was all in his head where he couldn't swat it away. And he had too much work to do to get drunk.

He let himself inside and found his way to Mike's office. Mike was a man with a very sedentary lifestyle and a gut to show for it. He looked sweaty, despite the cool air that circulated from his in-wall air conditioner. They got to talking briefly before Mike was interrupted with a phone call. He took it, hoping he could clear it up swiftly as his client sat in front of him.

Half an hour passed. Jake sat and waited patiently. He could tell there was a lot of pain going through Mike's head by the way he looked. It was like his toe was being forcefully impacted by a slow-moving plow like he was stubbing it over and over with every other word that came through the telephone.

"No, Mrs. Court," Mike explained. "We no longer use a fax

machine. All correspondence can be done via email or—or bring that lovely face of yours in the office." He was professional enough that his voice didn't have to match his expression. He sounded patient but looked exhausted. It was a kind of call he'd mastered after having it so many times before. "What's that? ….Okay, then, you do that. Thank you." He rushed to hang up the phone and sighed into his palms. He leaned back to compose himself and faced Jake with a slightly reddened face and sweaty forehead.

"Sorry about that, Mr. Campbell," he began again. He cleared his throat and resumed their conversation like no time had passed. "Yes. Like I was saying, your Mother didn't own the actual building. She was just leasing it running her business. I have the owners' flying in the next day or so to do an inspection."

Jake turned away to look out the window, past the air conditioner, to see what was going on outside. People were moving around. It made him nervous. The gang fallout from the other day still bothered him.

"No interest in taking over the Family Business yourself, Mr. Cambell?" Mike asked.

"Not planning on sticking around," Jake said, with a half-attentive answer. The phone rang again. Mike sighed. He checked the caller ID and sighed harder. Jake stood up and went to the other side of the office, where the window was unobstructed.

"Excuse me one moment, Mr. Campbell," Mike said as he picked up the phone. He opened his mouth to speak but was immediately interrupted by his caller. "Mrs. Court—okay. Yes….right, I see -."

While he went on, Jake inspected the outdoors. A window cleaner went by and squeegeed across the glass. The whole room seemed to brighten up as if the cleaning solution pried off a whole layer of sand. It gave Jake a better view of the outdoors and the people around. Mostly the gangsters from the other day. Based on how everyone described them to Natasha and explained their presence to him, he knew they were the main source of trouble at the bar.

Jake listened in slightly as the phone call ended and turned back to face Mike as he reached another exhaustive conclusion. "Sorry about that," Mike said. Jake looked back out the window. The window cleaner moved on, as did the gang members, off into the low profile of the city streets. "Can I help you with anything else today, Mr. Cambell?"

"That's it," Jake said. Their business was concluded, and Jake followed through with his part of the deal. With the last of the paperwork signed, the lease went up, and the pub lost its owners. Mike drove out later that same evening, once all the papers were squared away and digitized, to hammer in the FOR LEASE sign in front of the pub.

The inside was cleaned up over the course of the day, and all the intact pieces of the business were boxed up and ready to ship out. Jake did a lot of the heavy lifting. It was the one good merit he retained from his fighting career. He wasn't sore or old enough that he couldn't do some simple packing and lifting. And he had some help.

Sara was also working with him, making sure what was being packed up was worth keeping and taking away. Richard also helped stack things as much as he could, but he stayed distant from Jake. They worked on the same thing, separately, and didn't interact. At length, Richard retired first and set himself at the corner of the bar.

Jake managed a stack of boxes to keep them stable while Sara moved up behind him and kissed him on the cheek. He moved with her to the front door and held it open for her as she left. "I'm gonna miss working here," she said wistfully. She stepped out into the evening air and looked at the newly fixed sign next to the road. "If you need a hand moving stuff, just sing out."

"I'll take care of the rest," Jake said firmly. She smiled and turned away, leaving Jake with the shell of the pub he used to know, with nothing left to pack but the beer and the men inside. He let the door swing shut and returned to the darkened hall. He managed to pack away everything physical, but the memories were still too heavy to move.

And the embodiment of those memories sat at the end of the bar.

Chapter 13

R ichard rolled an old coaster around with his finger. The sight of the wheel spinning across a dust-speckled surface made him feel nostalgic. Then he reviewed the bar once more. The damage was all cleaned up, and everything was packed away. The pub he once knew was gone, first ruined by hostile hands and then taken over by greedier means.

Richard flipped the coaster over. There was a phone number on the back that he'd scrawled in while Jake was busy. He wanted to wait for Jake to approach him, but that didn't seem likely even when they were left completely alone. Jake went behind the bar and fetched one of the unpacked glasses from the wash bin. He cleaned it out and eyed the tap down, eager for a hard-earned drink.

Richard flicked the beer coaster down the bar. It got halfway before it teetered onto its side and fell flat, number side up. "Um," Richard began, "I'll leave it here."

Jake ignored his estranged father and poured himself a glass of beer. The pressure in the tap was low. It took long enough to fill the glass that Richard walked across the bar. The old man undid the clasp of his necklace and piled the thin leather stands on top of the coaster. In the center was a white rock, not clear enough to be a crystal, bound in a complex knot of leather string.

"This was a gift from your mother," Richard explained, "when we first dated many moons ago." he traced his fingers over it, just barely touching it with his dried, callused hands. Jake remained silent even after his father talked and only focused on his beer while Richard went on. "Free spirit, carefree, wild with a wicked sense of humor. You're my white knight. Sir Richard Lancelot, she'd call me." He chuckled lightly to himself at the memory. "Shame, because...because I...didn't, I couldn't live up to it. Hell, a white knight seemed too much for me to bear, to live up to, you know?"

Jake turned away from his beer and looked to the ground. It was obvious he wasn't tuning his father out anymore, but he couldn't bear to look straight at him.

"She had integrity!" Richard said, with heat and pain in his voice. "I got to say mine was compromised with all the other bullshit...I didn't see it at the time. I was young. I lost my way...." He took in a deep breath to compose himself, but it was a shaking, quivering breath. "Looking back, I can still see her mouthing the words...You're my White Knight." He started to cry. He whispered the words again, "You're my White Knight," as if he was racked with the pain of mighty blows. He stared deep at the rock in the necklace, all the memories fresh in his eyes. "The sweetest thing to ever be said to me."

Jake downed a throatful of beer and shook his head as it sank away into his gut. "So convenient for you," he said.

Richard looked up. The first words his son spoke directly

to him were layered with resentfulness. "Convenient?" he repeated.

"Taking off before the cops turned up yesterday," Jake explained.

Richard nodded. "I had my reasons," he admitted. "Besides, I haven't shown my face around here for years—Been laying low. I prefer people not knowing where I live."

"Nothing's changed," Jake said. He took the silence between them as an indicator to start drinking again, but he kept the glass tipped gently so he could stop at any moment.

"I was warned yesterday," Richard said. He leaned over the bar. "They're looking for AJ -."

"Do you really think," Jake interrupted, "I give a fuck about you and AJ and the rest of you animals -."

"He stole a large amount of cash," Richard said, "And we are family -."

"Family!?" Jake shouted. "You chose them as your family!"

Richard shook his head adamantly. "These people will kill anyone who stands in their way—that I know and I don't think it's -."

Jake hit his glass against the bar. The liquid inside jumped and jumbled in place. "You, along with the rest of these animals, can go to hell!" Jake stomped away from the bar to the front door. He jabbed his finger at the jukebox and sent the bar into total silence. Only the rattling of the glasses in the wash bin remained. Richard picked up the necklace and the coaster and walked over to Jake, who stood on guard—like he was facing an opponent.

"Your words mean shit!" Jake protested. "You would've been better honoring and staying with your real family. You can slowly rot and die in the arms of your brotherhood." Jake's words hit Richard like a stiff blow to the gut. He stopped just short of the door, then turned and slowly reached his hand forward. Jake saw it as a slow-moving punch—a faint to distract him. He lifted his arms to guard his face.

"I want you to keep this," Richard said. He held out the necklace in his hand. The leather straps drooped down over his palm.

Jake was confused and off guard. "Why even bother coming back here?"

Richard insisted on handing over the necklace. Jake took it. He saw Richard's forlorn expression as the rock left his possession. "You just never know when life's gonna hit you over the head. I wanted to come back and make amends with your Mother...but I was too late."

Richard turned to leave. He didn't look back, but his body language was that of a man who struggled to move forward. It was like he'd been struck out, knocked clean in the head, and his legs weren't listening to his rattled brain anymore. He was punch drunk with sadness. Jake leaned against the wall and inspected the pathetic keepsake in his hands. It was so light that he barely felt it at all.

He waited at the door until he heard the sound of an exposed motorcycle engine. The wall shook as it rumbled away. Jake crossed his arms and waited for the engine to fully fade out. He stood in the silence, his tinnitus replaced the sounds of his father's departure, and he leaned back against the wall in recollection.

He closed his eyes and thought back to what his father said. He had so many fond memories of her. It made Jake jealous and, once again, resentful, as he only had the worst memories of his dad...

Chapter 14

When Jake was just a small boy, about seven years old, his father brought him and his brother, AJ, to a biker's club. Jake would later learn that it was a strip club up front with a meth lab in the back. He sat in front of a blazing orange fireplace with a propane burner that chewed apart the carbon crust of the logs. He was huddled on the floor with his arms over his tucked-in knees.

"Boy," Richard said. He came up behind Jake and shook him gently with one hand. "Where's your brother?"

Jake turned to look up at his dad. He was dark from the club's underlit ceiling. Jake wanted to turn back to the comfortable sight of the flames. They looked hot and pleasant. Richard jerked Jake to the side again to address him.

"You're at the club now," he said gently. "What goes on here stays a secret. Nobody outside this club gets to know what we do. Not even mum—You understand?"

Jake stared up awkwardly. The flames in his eyes didn't go away. He watched as a topless woman snaked her arm around Richard's neck and pulled him away amorously. Richard turned to her with a smile and left Jake on the floor. His concern for AJ evaporated, gone like an ember that flickered off of the tip of the fire.

Jake took a deep breath in and expelled the memory. He opened his eyes in the present. He was abandoned again, in a far, sadder way. Instead of heading off to cheat with a whore, his dad left him with all he retained of his legacy as a family in his hand. He felt the necklace over again and gripped it tight.

He felt the emptiness of the room like a pressure. It was like walking through the halls in the back of a venue after a fight. All the excitement and dread were behind him. Victory or loss, winner or loser, the silence meant the fighting was over, and his body was awake for nothing. He was moving without purpose. He got trapped inside his head, with all the heat and pain and visions of the fire from his youth.

The only thing that grounded him was the necklace. He couldn't bear to drop it, and he felt like he could crush it if he got angry enough. It was firm but fragile in his grip. The safest place for it was around his neck. He tied it up and cinched it with a tiny metal clasp in the back. The sweaty leather drooped just above his chest. It fell higher on his tough frame than it did on his lanky, drained father's body.

Jake moved around through the pub and inspected everything. Soon it would be gone, and he would only be able to return as a patron, not even the familial stranger he came in as that week. There would be no more wandering behind the bar or into the upstairs. He had to do all of that while there was still time.

He headed into the back half of the building and entered his mother's room. The bed was covered with a miscellaneous mix of items. Some of them were even new. It was hard to believe that she was alive and sleeping in that bed just a few weeks ago. Days, even. Everything else was bundled up in cardboard boxes, all her clothes and other goods that no longer had an owner.

Sara didn't finish packing, by the looks of things. The items on the bed were all sentimental, precious things that only mattered to the family. Things like photo albums, framed pictures, and old school projects the kids made that their mother kept for decades. Jake picked up one of the old scrapbooks and saw old vacation photos, nature hiking souvenirs, and a whole page of old greeting cards he made as a kid with crayons and markers. Along with a message:

You're the best mum in the whole wide world, Love Jake

He put the album down gently and let it rest on the comforter. Like Sara must have done, he started to search through the books to rekindle his old memories. He found a picture of his high school days with Natasha, back when they were together, and thought they would stay together until they were old. Back when he lived his life for her and treated her like his whole world. Then it all just fell apart, and his rage took him in another direction.

He put the picture into a silver jewelry box with a few other photos and small trinkets like earrings, nose rings, bracelets, and necklaces. Jake palmed them over gently, but it slipped from his fingers. The box tilted off the nightstand and fell onto the floor with a harsh clatter as the small metal bits and bobs spread across the floor. A pearl necklace burst into pieces, and the smooth marble beads went everywhere.

Jake went down with a groan and picked up everything he could. It was the first time he'd been on his hands and knees in a while, for any reason. All he could think of was his ground game, his grappling and submission, and how swiping his hands surely had to be the quickest way to gather everything up. The beads scattered under the rug that was under the bed. Jake shot up and hoisted the bed out of the way to get to the rest of the stuff underneath. Most of the beads stopped rolling once they hit the rug, but a few went underneath.

He picked them up, one by one, and then rolled back the rug lengthways to get at the last few pearls. When he did, he saw something unexpected. Underneath his mother's bed was a trapdoor built into the floor, hidden by the rug. The latch was locked with a padlock carved down into the floor, with the keyhole away from him and fully stuck underneath the wood. It was locked in a way that even the proper key couldn't easily open.

Jake was a man of strength and resourcefulness. He wouldn't let any lock stand in his way. There was a secret in the house—his home—that he needed to uncover. His fingers couldn't reach the bottom of the lock. He needed something to pry it up, but even then, he still needed a key. Or, he needed the lock to be removed completely. The bolts of the latch were dead locked into the wood, no way to remove them. But the bar on the padlock was thin and old.

Jake went outside to a shed in the backyard. He brought a flash torch along to light the way and find what he was looking for. They had plenty of tools for the daily needs of the pub, as well as maintenance and general contracting type of work. He was familiar with all of them in passing. Growing up, either he or AJ had to do the heavy lifting and fixing to keep things running.

He scanned the wall and all its tools. They all looked dangerously overused. Saws with missing teeth, rusty wrenches, and a dark metal shovel hung side-by-side off the wall. At the end of the row was a pair of bolt cutters, heavy-duty. The kind they used to snip old valves from caskets for their aged imports. He picked them up and returned to the trap door. Breaking the lock took just two snips, and the metal band fell apart.

He lifted the latch over his head with ease and inspected the underside. Below his mother's bed were two black bags. He hoisted them out with his free arm and checked again. Nothing else. The compartment was just small enough to hide the bags and was lined with concrete. Not even mites could slip in. He turned his attention to the bags and unzipped them to see what was being hidden.

It definitely wasn't his mother's effects. One bag had a bundle of dollars—all hundreds. A glance told him there was over $100,000 in the bag, possibly multiple hundreds. That was sponsorship money. Title fight money, all in cash. He wasn't unfamiliar with the amount, but the packaging was new. When dealing with that amount, cash was never the safest route. Only criminals dealt with cash in such large bundles.

The other bag had less cash in it, bundled up like a layer, with several square butcher-paper packages wound tight with twine. The weight was deceivingly light. He guessed that there wasn't any meat inside. At the very bottom of the bag was a square tin cookie box. Jake shook it and heard something small but dense rattle inside. He popped open the top and saw a small cellphone, an old model with a newish exterior. He flipped it up, and, to his surprise, it lit up in response, with a meager amount of battery remaining.

Jake packed everything back up into the bags and stowed the bags back into the compartment in the floor. He covered the unsecured latch with the rug and moved the bed back on top of it all. He finished assembling all the lost gems into the jewelry box, set it on the nightstand, then lied down on the bed between the albums and knick-knacks.

His father's words rang hollow in his mind. There was crime afoot—literally, under his feet—in his own home. The time he spent away changed how his family lived. He felt even more distant from them than ever. He reclined and tried to relax with his eyes fixed on the ceiling. It felt different. Even though it was his home, the ceiling was unfamiliar. He felt like a stranger.

Instead of getting angry or sad, he got up to get a beer.

Chapter 15

Night in Silver City was dark. It wasn't a city in the traditional sense that city folk would know. After dark, most lights went out, and most businesses shut down for the day. Working after dark was something for essential staff or government workers. Even thieves had to sleep sometimes; those who worked at night would suffer during the day.

One place where work persisted after lights out was at the hospital. Richard sat in a sterile, white room in his boxers and a lead-lined apron. Behind him were a standing X-ray machine and a doctor who pinned the transparent printouts onto the backlit wall. They were shots of Richard's head. Part of the view from the top was obscured by a thin line from a long-healed fracture that reached from the back of his skull to the front.

A black spot was circled in the fleshy part of the brain. It was small but distinct, like an ink smudge on the paper but was definitely part of the brain. Richard glanced over his shoulder at the readouts and saw it. Seeing it made him seem to feel it in his head, like a heavy pea that rolled around on the interior of his skull.

The doctor huffed a sigh and held a bottle of pills out to

Richard before sitting down across from him on another examination stool. "Let's start you on these as from tonight," he instructed. "Let me know of any reactions that may occur during the night, and I will see you tomorrow for another session. Get some rest."

Richard nodded lethargically, like his head suddenly grew five times heavier, and gathered his clothes from the orange container in the corner. He was expected to somehow gain a positive rest after being given such distressing news and had to go out into the night to do it.

Meanwhile, other forces moved and worked in the darkness that was less reputable. A shadow moved outside of the pub and hung close to the window. Far in the back, Jake lounged back in a room with a canned beer in his hand, half-empty. He was ready to embrace the slow fall into sleep when he suddenly heard a loud barking sound from Max outside. The chained-up dog tugged at the limit of his chain lead with snapping, growling jaws.

Jake sprung up and ran into the main room. He saw the shadow move toward the door, and then it was replaced with a loud knocking at the main entrance. Jake marched over, fully awake and just drunk enough to swing straight to the front door. He checked who was on the other side. The first thing he saw was the uniform, local police. He unlocked the door and let Harvey in, out of the dismal evening humidity and away from Max.

Jake leaned out of the door and nodded to the loyal guard dog. "Good boy," he said. Max sat and panted with his tongue flapping in the air. Harvey took a relieved breath and shook off the startle that the dog gave him. Jake closed the door behind him and took a sip of beer.

"Phew!" Harvey exclaimed. "Mighty big dog." He heard Max growl in response to his voice. He continued, in a lower tone, to Jake. "Good to have some protection out here." Jake tipped the can up nearly vertical and finished it off while giving Harvey a distrustful side-eye. Harvey acknowledged the wordless dismissal with a chuckle and rubbed his hands together. "Look, I'm sorry it's late. You don't mind?"

Jake tilted his head curiously and loudly gulped his beer down with force. Harvey nodded and took it as an intimidating acknowledgement. "I just wanted you to know," the officer began, "if you need any help, my door is always open." Jake smirked, still hanging onto his distrusting leer. "It's a peaceful town. Want to keep it that way." Jake nodded along with a sarcastic grin on his face. "If there is anything out of the ordinary, you can tell me."

Jake sized Harvey up like he would a fighter from the opposite corner. He was a rugged-looking man, but the years behind the desk seemed to dull his sharper edges. He had the body and posture of a fighter. Even when he was relaxed, he looked ready to spring to attention and fight at the first sign of trouble. He projected a heavy aura of authority and a will to enforce it. Like he was the one looking for trouble just for the chance to take control of it. Harvey read Jake the same way and reached his own conclusion with a smirk.

"Good," he said. "Okay, that's all really. Just to welcome

you. And, enjoy your stay." Harvey swayed to the door and let himself out. Jake watched him leave while he crushed the empty can in his hand. Jake watched out the window as Harvey avoided Max and went straight for his car across the road. Harvey turned and saw Jake in the window. He nodded his head down, gentlemanly, and got in his patrol car. Once it was gone, peace returned to the empty night outside.

Jake never had the best luck with cops. He was a big man whose life revolved around violence. He was an easy target for controversy, always had been. Even as a kid, he was a tough rebel. He was used to scrutiny from officers in the past, but not such critical judgement. It felt like the moments before a major fight, where his opponent was trying to read his first moves before the introductions were over.

He felt hot and heavy. The rush of bursting through the pub as fast as he could to catch an intruder left adrenaline pooling in the back of his skull. He felt sick and wobbled back to his room in the back to rest for the rest of the night, no more drinking and no more danger. He trusted Max more than a cop to protect him. Especially one that made night calls when most people would be out robbing the closed down, unlit businesses in town.

Chapter 16

Morning came. It was hot and dry. Jake woke up in a slow stupor at first, but then his athletic mind took over. He had a routine, even on break. Even after a tragedy, he had to get moving. He had to run. He suited up with jogging pants and a sleeveless tank top with his old branding on it. A classic piece of merch with sleeves torn off, and the dark colors were one shade darker from the years of sweat stains.

He greeted Max outside, filled up his food bowl, patted him on the head, then picked a direction and started jogging. The sun was still rising. The chill of the night lingered in the air. He was early enough to beat the wild inland Australian heat halfway through his jog. Then the sun started to rise. He faced away from it and started to jog back. Half an hour out of town and half an hour back in. A few cars passed him out on the long, dirt road to nowhere. One of them was a cop car, which inspired Jake to pick up his pace a little.

The hard dirt ground had a different feel to the concrete tiles in the city or the tarmac tracks in his usual gym. It was softer, had a different give to it. When he ran, he attacked the ground below him for explosive strength and tested his legs and ligaments with every step. Without the need to fight and removed from his environment, he felt like his motions were all wrong. He had to move in a more relaxed manner to stay in line with the dirt. Being home made him softer, the difference between processed material and raw Earth.

The patrol car drove up beside him. He stiffly ignored it at first. The window rolled down, and he dared to take a glance. He assumed he'd see Harvey, so he prepared a stern glare but was pleasantly surprised to see Natasha instead.

"You need a lift?" she asked.

"I get nervous in cop cars," he immediately jested. Natasha smiled.

"I wouldn't want that," she said.

"I'd feel a whole lot better," he mentioned between his breaths, "chatting over a beer."

"I'd feel a whole lot better drinking out of this uniform," she replied.

"Well, you know where you can find me."

Natasha gave a sincere grin and leaned back in her seat. "Then I'll see you later tonight?"

"Okay," Jake said. "Sure." She rolled up her window and rolled away. Jake felt revitalized in his run. He got his second wind early and expended his excess excitement with some shadow boxing on his way back into town. His pace sped up, but his speed stayed the same. Shorter steps, more like hops, in time with the rest between each swing. He punched through the air until he was back at the pub.

He gave himself a long cooldown with a shower and a meaty breakfast to replace his burnt-out proteins. Jake ate at the bar, on the opposite side, acting as an off-shift bartender would. It wasn't his pub, but it was his home. With the business suspended, the bar effectively served as one long dining table. Midway through, as he munched on a link of sausages, he got a phone call on his mobile again. He answered it at the same time that a man entered the front door. Jake looked up, expecting a confused drunk who couldn't read the signs out front.

"Hello?" Jake said quietly. His ears were open, but his eyes and other senses were fixed on the gangster that moved into the bar. He wore a bandana over his face and had dark, gritty hair. He shuffled his way up to the bar with a lazy gait.

"Jake?" It's AJ…."

"Where are you?" Jake demanded.

"Come meet me now at the white quarter-mile," AJ said. He hung up. Jake put his phone down behind the bar and moved to intercept the man who took a seat.

"We're closed," Jake demanded. The gangster looked over his shoulder. His eyes were combative and hateful, but his tone was sarcastic.

"The door was open," he said.

"Business is closed," Jake said adamantly.

"Six-pack will do me fine -."

"You hard of hearing?" Jake shouted. "Closed."

The gangster sprung up and prodded his finger at Jake's

chest. "You have a hearing problem? Six. Pack. Asshole!"

Jake asserted himself again. He pushed his chest up to crowd the guy out. It was like a handshake for ring fighters. A butting of heads to prove they were ready to do battle. The honorless, uncoordinated, sloppy gangster didn't have the same ritual. As soon as Jake got too close, he faded back with a swing. A slow, pathetic swing in Jake's eyes. He saw it coming what felt like minutes in advance, which gave him plenty of time to visualize his opening maneuver.

Jake jerked his arm up and intercepted the flying fist with the tip of his elbow, interior, right at the angle where he felt nothing. His ulnar nerve—the funny bone—was unaffected. The gangster's fist was sealed. His fingers were bruised and probably broken. The pain rocked the man into a stagger backwards as he clutched his throbbing hand. Jake closed the distance in one step with his arms down in a grappling position. He swiped his arms up, grabbed the man by the back of his shoulders, and tore him down. The gangster lost his balance and fell onto his back.

Jake was on him immediately with a flurry of blows. He threw soft hooks and stiff straights at his face, just enough to faze him. Once the man brought his fists up to defend himself, Jake went back to grappling. His thick leather jacket made it easy to hold on to. It wasn't like dealing with a sweaty body that could slip and wriggle away. The man was essentially wearing bondage gear that kept him tied up under Jake's control.

As far as an official match went, the fight was already over in less than a minute. Eight seconds to put the guy on the ground from the bell, and he was already cowering. He'd given up in his heart but didn't know the signal. And since Jake saw no signal and heard no bell, he kept going. He was in fight mode. He was Raging. He grabbed the man's arm and spun off his chest to put it between his thighs at an angle. The gangster started screaming as he felt his arm get twisted like licorice.

Jake looked up. He searched for searing overhead lights or a ref in a bright white jumper. He saw none of that. He remembered where he was in an instant. The floor wasn't a solid, springing mat. It was hardwood and dust. He saw the hand clutching in pain, twisted around so far it looked backwards. He let the gangster go and reverse-rolled over his head back onto his feet. Jake sprung up in a low stance, ready to grab again, while his victim laid on the floor, reeling in pain.

He was an amateur fighter. Whatever skill gave him that leather jacket wasn't born from one-on-one fighting. Jake handily won and stood up, victorious but disappointed. It felt like he was a trainer, teaching some upstart kid just how weak and pathetic he was compared to a real fighter. No honor and no real victory at all. All he managed to do was make a biker shed tears of pain.

He felt like a proper bouncer.

Chapter 17

Gavin rolled up in his white Holden Ute with a sleek Scrambler YZ 250 dirt bike tied up on the back. The whole car shifted a little as it stopped. The brakes needed an extra foot to make a full stop. Gavin sat back and leaned his elbow out the window as he waited in front of the pub. Just a minute or so later, the pub's front door swung open, and Jake came out with a heavy load dragging behind him. Gavin did a double-take when he saw it. He thought it looked like a body.

It was. A moving one, though. Jake hoisted the crumpled gangster up by his collar and threw into the dirt away from the sidewalk. The gangster rolled around in a daze and slowly picked himself up. He tried to use his right hand, but the shooting pain in his shoulder forbade him from moving it. It also woke him the whole way up to see Jake standing over him.

"Get the hell out of here," Jake warned. The biker whimpered, jumped up, and ran for his bike. He winced and shouted as he turned over the engine and used his limpish arm to work the throttle. He tore away down the road in a panicked flight while Jake stood by. Once the thug was out of sight, Jake turned his attention to the Ute and its driver. Gavin leaned his head out the window.

"Heard you were back in town," Gavin called.

Jake nodded to Gavin and headed over to his Mustang. "I had reason to this time," he said. He looked his car over quickly in a slow gait, then rushed over to the passenger side tire. "Ah shit." The tire was flat to the ground.

"Got a flat one there?" Gavin asked. He exited his truck and inspected the scene beside Jake. They both found the culprit, a stray nail stuck out of the side, slightly exposed, and worked up to the head into the rubber. Jake turned with a soft, boiling fury to Gavin, who smirked back. "Where you heading?"

Jake turned, about to shake his head over the prospect of asking for a ride. He was about to deal with a family matter— a private one—and didn't want to drag someone unsuspecting into it. Then he saw the bike.

"That thing goes?" Jake asked.

Gavin turned to the bike. "Like lightning," he bragged.

"Mind if I borrow it?" Jake asked.

Gavin patted Jake on the shoulder. "Needs some juice. Hop in." Jake beat Gavin to the truck and strapped in before Gavin got to his door. Gavin made a pointing gesture down the road where the biker fled. "What the fuck happened with him?"

"Don't look too good, does he?" Jake said with a dark boast. Gavin tried to match the mood with an unsure grin. "He'll be fine. Let's go." Gavin remained suspicious but maintained his composure to help his longtime friend out. He shifted to first and rolled away with the bike in the back, waiting for Jake's use.

The ride up was quiet. Jake didn't want to say what he was doing, just that he couldn't wait for a car repair and walking was too far. It was an emergency, and when Gavin tried to pry, he got a disquieting look, like even Jake was afraid to speak of it. They rolled up to the last petrol station out of Silver City, in the direction Jake needed to go.

Gavin unstrapped the bike from the holsters while Jake pushed it over to the pumps to fill it up. He reached into his pocket just as Gavin came over to ask the inevitable. The gas was Jake's treat, with change. "Fill it up, buddy," Gavin said. He waved the thin wad in his hand. "I'll go pay." Jake nodded while Gavin headed for the station.

The bike had a small, simple engine but enough power to tear through the wasted ground and thick layers of sand that covered the landscape just out of town. That was its specialty. It was an offroader, and Jake had to meet AJ far off the beaten road. The white quarter mile was in the shallows of a former salt lake, a place not even lizards wanted to live. The seconds of filling the tank up felt like minutes passing under the hot morning sun. While Jake did that, Gavin went in to pay, but first, he hid in an aisle and talked in hushed tones on his mobile.

"Head over straight away," was all he said out of a whisper. He hung up the phone and grabbed a beer for the road. He set it down in front of the apathetic cashier, then looked out the window as Jake just got done hanging up the nozzle into the bowser. "And the petrol," he added. The attendant rang it up with ease.

Jake peered in just to make sure the sale went through.

From his vantage point, he saw behind the attendant and caught a glimpse at a wanted poster. For Vehicle Manslaughter. Any information, et cetera. With a familiar, aged-up face of his brother up top. Jake ran over to kick start the bike. Gavin came out with his beer and change just before the first chug of the engine kicked over.

"Wait here," Jake said. "I won't be long." He dropped the clutch and zipped forward with impressive speed. His bike whirred and whined up the road toward the empty salt lake basin and the long road around it. Gavin stood by near his car and entertained himself by sipping on his beer. If he had to wait, he wanted a cool throat when his guest arrived.

Chapter 18

The thug Jake thrashed drove out of town to the hidden away clubhouse, a quick sprint for a bike of his power. He felt burning pain every time he twisted the throttle. Every muscle in his arm felt like it was on fire and full of needles. The back of his head hurt, too, as did his shoulder blades. His left fist, which he swung into Jake's elbow, was just as pained, and he couldn't uncurl it out of a fist. He gritted his teeth to bear the pain but lapsed into frightful sobs every couple hundred yards down the road.

He rolled up to the garage where the other members were working out. They had a sandbag for boxing and gave freelance fighting tips to each other. It was a rough, disorganized sort of gym atmosphere. Men were practicing, making motions and poses from traditional martial arts branches. The Asian members were doing the physical teaching, and the caucasian members followed along or pressed weights made of dismembered bike parts to get stronger.

Meanwhile, the rest of the members were working. They maintained the bikes and filled tanks up with stolen petrol. A row of dirt bikes was on the main floor, separate from the bigger choppers and offroaders. The members who weren't working with spanners and drills stood by on a smoke break instead.

Everyone turned when they heard the motorcycle roll up. The driver, Jake's victim, lowered the kickstand and nearly fell off from the delirious pain he was in. A few guys rushed over to check him—though most were concerned for his bike. They turned the engine off while he sank to his knees and started to crawl. One of the guys took his bandana off and saw a polka-dot pattern of bruises and bloody marks from Jake's fast rain of blows.

"Bit of an accident?" the gangster said. "Fall off ya bike?" The sarcasm didn't sit well with the tortured soul. He started blabbering and blithering nonsense words, but a few came through loud and clear.

"The pub….some guy….fucking *Brutal!*"

One guy did all that to him, and he was no weakling. None of them were. They all took a step back and reviewed their workouts as if the revelation that there were fights they couldn't just walk up and win was shockingly brand new. Amid their little confidential upheaval, Tony walked out to see what was going on. He saw the injured member on the ground and went up to meet him. The beaten guy stood up and shook his head to try and straighten himself out in front of the boss.

"What happened to you?" Tony asked. He tilted his head around and analyzed the thug like he was inspecting a used car for parts.

"That prick at the pub," he said. "The Brother. Whacked me a good one, so me and the boys we're heading back to give him a beating." The boys he referenced stood at attention for approval. None of them agreed to that, but in the face of their boss, they knew they couldn't. One by one, they started cheering, mostly with slurs directed at the attacker.

"Jake?" Tony said. The thug nodded. Tony grabbed him by his bad shoulder. Pain dropped the thug's mouth wide open. "I told you to keep a fucking eye out—not engage!" He stopped shaking his injured crew. As soon as he let go, the man dropped down and clutched his broken fingers at his torn shoulder on the ground. Tony took a breath and calmed himself, then turned to the boys in wait and addressed them. "Don't worry about that. Follow me. Got a location on AJ's whereabouts."

The team assembled and went for their bikes. Some climbed on heavy choppers. Others took the most recently renovated dirt bikes. All of them left their injured comrade behind. Tony led the brigade as they rolled out from their headquarters and made a dash to cut across Silver City and cut Jake off from his brother. AJ was wanted by more than just the police. He was the target of all the most dangerous animals in the wastelands.

Chapter 19

A band of white dust kicked up from the rear tire of a bike as it ripped across the expanses of the salt lake flats. A long rider stood out as a roving disturbance on the horizon. He was far out enough that he couldn't see the road. He was hidden from sight only by heat shimmers miles away.

He found his way to the sloping, eroded shoreline and ramped up an incline to the roadway above. The long way around the salt flat was marked by packed down brown in the reddish surrounding dirt. A few scrub plants rose to meet him. He stepped off the bike and lifted his helmet off his face to get a few unimpeded breaths.

AJ was the spitting image of Jake, just a bit younger and thinner. He traded Jake's hard and heavy figure for a more streamlined, fit, but well-fed proportion. He was strong enough to work on his bike and do meager menial work, not to fight and win like a rampaging behemoth. AJ crouched down next to his bike and went over his options in his head. He trusted his brother to meet him but knew there were others. The next sound of a bike he heard would either be salvation or something worse than dying in the middle of the heated fields.

He stood up once he heard it. The bike whined like a

braying horse as it trembled along the dirt path. AJ's eyes started to tear up from a rush of emotions as Jake arrived, alone and unstopped.

Jake scanned the distance for a sign of his brother. He was at the right spot, the quarter-mile stretch of white beach along the dried-up lake. His eyes were fixed on the wide flatland at first. Then he saw the figure standing at the side of the road. He hoped it was AJ when he slowed himself to a stop but remained unsure until he saw his brother's face- the same face from the poster, but grateful instead of scowling.

Jake got off his bike and caught it before it fell. AJ came up to him while he worked the kickstand and immediately embraced his brother just as the bike found solid ground. "It's good to see you," AJ said. He sucked up some of his sadness and stepped away. He wasn't done crying, but he pushed a smile through to greet his brother properly.

Jake wasn't as grateful or happy or emotional at all. He was worried and stern. He lightly gripped AJ by his shoulders and gave him a gentle rocking. "What the hell happened, AJ?" he asked. AJ could tell there was a lot to unpack in his question. It sounded like he knew a lot, but not enough.

"Mum and I were heading out late ah," he began, with a nervous tic punctuating his story. "We ah had dinner ah she wanted to drive she loved driving—I let her of course, and ah out of nowhere lights shone from the front of us bikes speed up from the rear we got ambushed, and she lost control of the car and...happened so fast. I tried to wake her. She was dead." He swallowed. His mouth suddenly dried out, like the long haul across the salt plain finally caught up to him. "I could see they were coming back -I got out. I hid."

"You're up for Manslaughter," Jake warned. "Whole town's looking for you."

AJ shook his head. The panic was rising in his eyes. "No, no, you see...I watched them drag mum out, and they placed her in the passenger's side made it look that way. That image of them torching the car is forever burnt into my fucking skull." He started to sob. "Of course, the whole town is looking for me." He fell forward into Jake's shoulder. Jake held him close. "We were planning to leave this town behind, mum and I—for good. Start new."

"Is that why you stole the cash?" Jake asked.

AJ sniffled and stepped away. "We both needed it," he confessed.

Jake pitied his brother. He wasn't angry, but his face was upturned with an expression of disappointment. It was like sizing up an opponent he knew was far, far under his league but that he had to fight for promotional purposes. It was a look of shame that AJ seemed to interpret well but resisted. AJ was adamant about his position and justified. He returned Jake's smoldering look with cold insistence, which was made even harsher by the glimmer around his eyes from his tears. Jake didn't like it, but AJ knew he was in the right.

The sound of the wind between them was interrupted by a distant rumble of engines. They turned toward the road where Jake came from and saw a cloud of dust heading their way. Jake stepped forward to inspect the procession. It was the gang members, the same ones who wrecked the bar, led by one man on a vicious-looking bike with long handlebars and a deep-lean seat.

"Meet me at the pub tonight," Jake demanded. "Get out of here, now!"

AJ nodded. He slapped on his helmet and tore out down the road away from the arriving gangsters. Jake moved his loaner bike to the side and stood beside it, blocking as much of the road as he could. He stood firm with his arms crossed and his feet light. He was no fool. He knew he couldn't stop a bike in a head-on collision. But they couldn't risk losing their bikes in a pileup or running a daisy-chain of recovery with their bounty taking the lead.

The lead bike sped by fearlessly. He passed Jake without so much as grazing the man, just off the beaten road. AJ gained distance rapidly, and the roadster bike struggled against the soft sands at the edge of the salt flats. They left Jake behind in a plume of dust that quickly settled and gave his hair a light frost of reddish sand.

He looked like he was glowing orange, with embers of an old fire still licking away at his edges.

Chapter 20

The four thugs that followed Tony all slowed down. They failed to gauge the distance as their boss could. Their eyes weren't as keen, and their vision couldn't account for the speed between them. They all stopped a few meters short of Jake and got off their bikes to move him by force. Their bandanas were skull patterned as if enough to mask their personalities and give them some kind of power boost.

"Well, well," one familiar voice said. "Look what we got here." Jake recognized the member by his wild eyes and pained voice. The member he dealt with earlier was back. His shoulder was wrapped up heavy and taped up in a botched-looking compression job. He moved around like he was out of sorts like he was high enough not to feel the pain.

The other three started to slowly crowd around Jake while their vengeful friend walked up and looked past him. "Likes a game of hide and seek—your brother?" he asked. Jake didn't give him any indication, not even in his eyes. He didn't even flinch when the man jerked forward to headbutt Jake in the face. Jake took it right in the nose. It was a forceful blow. He stepped back a few times—not in a stumble, but a collected retreat.

"When I ask for a beer," the gangster shouted, "I get beer, you hear!" Jaked raised his head and held it back for a second. He could hear his opponent grind at the ground in preparation to charge. Jake took a long breath of hot, dry air in, then lowered his face and burst it out through his nostrils. A few flecks of blood splattered out and hit his shirt collar. The sight stunned the gangster half-step into his charge, just within Jake's reach.

Jake flicked his waist. His right arm jabbed as he stepped forward. It was just a tap, but it was startling. Then he connected a left hook as he planted his right foot, a solid blow. It pushed the gangster back. With his right foot forward and right arm wound tight to his side, Jake pivoted with his heel and twisted his body, delivering a powerful straight to the thug's face in a step-in karate style corkscrew.

The thug went down. He stayed down, even as the members gathered around to goad him up. They looked up at Jake with fear. They didn't even see the first punch he made. He stepped forward and rested with the corner of his heel in the dirt, both hands up in a loose, ungripped formation. It looked like he stopped in place before he finished getting ready. One of the thugs took that as an indication to attack.

Jake finished his kata with the same fluid quickness and snapped a punch at the charging thug's face. Right above the nose, at the eyes. His opponent blinked instinctively. Jake planted his left foot and jabbed with his right knee, right under the ribs. The man bent over, breathless. Jake grabbed him by the back of the head and flicked his wrist down. The man fell straight forward onto his face and rested, butt up, knocked out on the ground.

"You suck," Jake sighed. The other two attacked together. Just what Jake wanted them to do. He swung his leg and toppled the fallen bandit over at the thug on his right, tripping him with his own friend. He stumbled out of the way toward the shoulder of the road, which gave Jake just enough time to slug the other man. He came in swinging. Jake blocked with his arm then slid forward. The man's fist got pushed back mid-blow, and he was off-balance. Jake wrapped his arms around the guy's neck and shoulder-checked him in his covered jaw. There was minimal risk of a biting attack since he was kind enough to wear a mask.

One opponent remained. He regained his footing just in time to see his friends get bodied. Jake turned his way. He could see the gears turning. The thug went through several upper guard boxing poses and put his right foot forward. He was readying a mixed approach, strikes up front and leg sweeps down below. His stance was basic but refined. Overall he looked like he knew what he was doing.

Jake felt the heat. The salt flats ahead of him were like a giant, searing stadium light, bright white and blazing to the touch. There was just one shadow in his way. He put his arms up the same way. His opponent countered with a lower stance, drawn back, more defensive. Jake opened his hands and lowered his arms. The thug didn't know how to deal with that. He was used to striking random people, not so much fighting as smacking odd civilians around.

No casual practitioner or criminal fighter was ready for a professional ground fight. Jake rushed in low. His whole body went under the thug's middle line—where his belt would be in a proper ring. Jake made a lunging grab for the man's legs. The thug tried to swing at the back of Jake's head but missed and ended up pressing fist against Jake's solid back. The tackle connected. Jake clasped his hands, cinched his opponent tight, and whipped his body forward, head toward the ground, which threw the man's body down like a big wet sack.

The third thug that got the shoulder check stood up and roared as he charged Jake down. Jake held his first opponent to the ground and waited until he was about to be pounced on. He could tell his opponent had no plan but to try and pound at his back or legs from behind. He waited until the thug got close, pushed up off the ground, and donkey-kicked him in the groin. He took the blow and fell backwards. The fourth thug started to squirm, so Jake mounted him and started raining blows on his face.

After a dozen hits, the man stopped resisting. It took a dozen more for Jake to notice. He stood up slowly and surveyed the results of his multi-man exhibition match. Four down, and he was still standing with nothing but sore knuckles to take home. No title, no prize. Judging by their bikes, not even a better ride. He looked back down the road and saw the dust clouds of the chase in the distance recede away into the heat shimmers of the afternoon sun.

He mounted his bike and sped back up the road. He trusted AJ to avoid trouble for just one more hour. And when he did, he'd need a stiff drink from a nice, warm tap to celebrate. First, he had to get back to town. He drove the bike up a shade redder than when he left to the petrol station, but Gavin's Ute was nowhere to be seen. He drifted to a stop just to make sure it wasn't pulled around or up the road, but it was strictly gone. The attendant at the bowser even gave Jake an uncertain shrug.

Jake kicked off and rode back up the road. Town was close enough that the bike on a full tank could still make it. He hoped AJ would make it too, considering he might be light on petrol after his long ride across the flats....

Chapter 21

A J rocked on his bike seat over the hard road. He was getting into the rough patch, meant for big cars with heavy wheels. His dirt bike's suspension struggled to stay intact. It was doing far better than Tony's bike. He didn't come fully prepared. His lowriding hog shuddered against the rocky terrain. The salty biker gritted his teeth under his bandana and squinted raw, hateful beams at AJ's back as the runner pulled away.

As long as they were on the road, AJ would be vulnerable. Even if he kept the pace up and evaded Tony, one of their gas tanks was bound to give, and his was smaller. AJ made a daring move and veered into a scrub patch. His bike fit through the thistles and other scruffy bushes with ease. The rough terrain was perfect testing for the shock pads on his bike, better than the rapid vibrations of the hardened road. He was off-road, a place Tony knew he couldn't follow.

"Fuck!"

Tony skidded to a stop and angled his bike for a return trip up the main road. He watched as AJ went from a stream of dust to occasional coughs of soil out of the packed down earth. There was no straight path for Tony's road-loving bike to follow. He lost AJ's trail but made the best guess as to his next move. They both had a long road to follow to get back to town on time.

Time passed. In the evening, only one motorcycle rode through Silver City, searching for the once-established pub. The former heir and never owner sat outside fixing the tire on his Mustang that was already covered up to the skirting with a layer of sticky dust. Jake arrived with enough presence of mind to pass his time on errands while he waited for his wanted brother to roll in. He trusted him and felt like his trust was being stretched thin with each passing minute.

He got the busted tire off and loaded it into the boot, then swapped it with the spare while his car was tilted up on the jack. After the fights he had, the droning manual labor did a lot to calm his mind. He didn't have to think about how best to break and cripple a car. He could fix something instead of just tearing it up with his inner rage.

After fixing his car, he went back inside and lounged in the bar room with the music on. The setlist was the same as always, but the box itself was updated. The bar's newest and most expensive piece of unbroken merchandise was a simple, digital living room jukebox. The kind he could have picked up on a drunken bender with a fraction of his former paycheck, then break open the next day with a bottle through the open face glass case.

Jake sat and drank a bottle of Jack, his only friend in rough times. It was halfway done, or only half started. He skulled down a few swigs, then suddenly couldn't keep it down. He started huffing the liquid out like he was coughing. When he brought the bottle away from his mouth, he discovered—to his own surprise—that he was sobbing. He was so distracted by his sudden lapse of attitude he didn't notice the sound of a bike engine pulling up or hear someone enter the main room of the pub or see who it was until they made a charge at him.

"Jake?" Richard said. "Jake!" he said again, with an airy voice of concern. Jake remained head-down and broken up. Richard reached forward to stir Jake from his drunken state. The soft-touch was enough to send Jake from one end of his emotional extremes to the other. He quickly held the bottle in an overhand grip and reeled it up to smash it. Richard backed away in time to miss the attack.

"Take your fucking hands off me!" Jake hollered. He didn't even notice who it was for another moment. When he did, he felt no shame, only more rage welling up—covering him like a swell of water smothering the bottom of a dried-out lake bed.

"Looks like you've had one too many, son," Richard said, attempting to be placative.

"I'm just getting started," Jake said. He flipped the bottle back over, not noticing that the rest of it was spilled around his feet. "Have one with your…. *Son*."

Richard kept his hands up and stood a few steps back while Jake sloppily advanced. All of his fighting acumen and posture were gone, but his strength remained. Richard shook his head politely. "Going on eight years now—sober." Jake smashed his hands together, still holding the bottle in mock applause. "Look, maybe I'll come back when you're sober."

Jake stomped to a stop. He stood like he was about to fall over like his left arm weighed a hundred pounds more than his right. "You hate me, don't you?"

Richard turned from his retreat and faced Jake sincerely. "What? No."

"Yes, you do," Jake said in a dark, low tone. "You've always hated me."

Richard shook his head, unable to assuage Jake's rising distrust. "Listen, son. The drink has you -."

"Has me what?" Jake asked.

"Nothing," Richard insisted. "You're just a bit drunk, that's all."

"You know what it has me?" Jake said. Richard clasped his mouth shut and let Jake go on. "Has me thinking that I don't even really know you. Has me thinking, who the fuck are you? You were never around. I'm back here looking across at you, and I see nothing. But that's ok. So I don't need you to be here. You can go."

Richard faced Jake's deep, scathing verbal beating and stayed standing. Jake threw out his best haymakers and knee-bucklers, but the old man stayed put. "Okay," Richard said, "What if I don't want to go?"

Jake sneered. "Fine. I'll leave. I'm heading back, getting out of here."

"You can't be driving like this -."

"Hello?" Natasha called from the shuttered window. "Jake?"

Jake and Richard were both distracted for a moment. They turned at the same time with something to say. Rage rose in Jake's throat, threatened to choke him unless he could spit it all out at once.

"I'm sorry," Richard said. The rage stopped, and Jake listened. "For not being around. For not being a decent father. That's why I came here." Richard turned on his heel and moved for the front door. He opened it up and greeted the surprised Natasha.

"Hello Richard," she said. "Oh, don't need to leave cause I'm here."

"No, that's fine," Richard said politely. He stepped outside and replaced Natasha across the threshold. "I best be going. Just happy he has some decent company." Jake made his way across the floor and met Natasha at the door in his half-lidded, stupored state. Richard fished in his pocket for a key ring and pulled one off with some extra effort from his weak fingers.

He held out a key on a smaller ring to Jake. "Spare key to my pad," he said gently. Jake turned his head away in rejection. Richard paused, seeing that his son wouldn't take it, and he looked up. He placed the key above the door on a hook next to the wind chime on the porch. If he wouldn't take it, then it would stay there for everyone else to see, another knick-knack bedazzled on the headboards of the old pub. Jake stared off into the distance, ignoring the key. Natasha stood between them in the doorway and looked over Richard with a puzzled expression.

"Make sure he don't drive tonight," Richard whispered.

"Oh, that won't be happening," Natasha confirmed.

Richard winked at her and gingerly fled to his motorcycle. Once he was on and got it started, Natasha turned to tend to Jake. "Let's go inside," she insisted. Jake looked past her. He saw the cloud of dust his father left behind, proof that he was abandoning Jake yet again. Jake looked over his Mustang and his body followed through. He got halfway down the porch before Natasha grabbed his wrist from behind. "No, Jake!"

Richard left the town behind and didn't check his mirrors. He was sure his son was safer without him, at least for the time, and in the company of someone he trusted. Richard's Harley rumbled and thundered across the wide, flat outback roads that led away from Silver City. He got behind and confidently overtook a white Ute with straps across the back that was driving straighter than it had to.

Gavin, tipsy behind the wheel, heard the motorcycle overtake him before he saw it. His hands clutched the wheel tight, and his eyes widened. He scanned over the make and model of the bike to see if he recognized it, but he didn't. It was a stranger's bike in a town where every biker knew each other. And he was just following the one outlier down a long, dark road....

Chapter 22

Jake felt a shifting, shaking sense of lost balance. Everything was cold and dark. His stomach was turned, and his head swam. It felt like he'd been combo'd, one to the gut and one to the chin, the kind of mix-up that meant he was on a quick course to losing.

He realized he wasn't in a ring of any kind, no walls or grates or fencing. He was in his car, which meant he had to do some driving. That's what made sense to him. He fumbled to get his keys out of his pocket as Natasha gripped at his shoulder to tug him away.

"Jake, you're drunk!" she exclaimed. He barely heard her. She was just part of the crowd, in the stands, watching him tumble. He put the keys in and cranked the engine. It came to life with a loud, satisfying thunder. He pressed on the pedal, still in park, and revved the engine more. He liked the way it sounded.

"Jake, please!" Natasha shouted. "Stop it!" He revved again and prepared to set off. "Jake, it's illegal to drive!"

"Oh right," Jake shouted back, over the sound of the engine, with his foot still lazily depressed on the pedal. "Because you're the law, right? You're a cop, right!? You have the power, right!?"

He looked over at her, combative, and got hit with her pleading expression, not in any position to fight back. "If you ever cared one bit about me, Jake," she said, "you wouldn't do it."

Jake felt the numbing vibrations of the car beneath him and slowed them down. He took his pedal off the gas and hiked his foot up into the footwell again. He turned the car off with a sigh and let the keys jingle. The loud thrumming noise bored through his head and brought him back to the quiet reality of Silver City, where he was the loudest thing for miles in those moments.

"Thank you," Natasha sighed.

Jake leaned back and sat in his seat in total silence. His feelings of lightheadedness and flighty ambition were replaced with anger and a bit of shame. He reflected on the things he's said and done, specifically to her, and all the things he still had left to say.

He turned to her in the silence and broke it. "Where were you the night of the accident?"

Natasha turned and looked him over. His neck drooped, and his posture slouched, he looked like he was asking for a bedtime story, but the question brought up sad things which couldn't make for any pleasant dreams.

"I happened to be out of town with mum," she admitted. "Why?"

"Because," Jake began, turning his head around, "all I see around this Town are Posters posters of my Brother accused and wanted for Murder. How so?"

"Well," she began, "what my fellow officers Charlie and Harvey have told me, it had been reported that night that a witness saw your Brother," she paused and adjusted her tone, as if reading from an official report dressed down to be more tasteful for the bureaucratic minded, "move your mother."

Jake looked at her, half sick but all curious. "From the driver's side into the passenger's side—ran away while she burnt? Just left her there."

She nodded. "Pretty much what I was told."

"Told," Jake said. "I was told a different version." He lifted himself over the convertible door and stumbled to his stance. He headed inside. Natasha quickly followed.

In no time, Jake set up a game of billiards while Natasha set the mood for the room at the jukebox. He lined up a shot and broke the balls in a swift thrust. Natasha stood by and let a sad ballad play out while she searched through the catalog on the box. She was on her second pass-through. Despite the sounds of music and clacking balls, the silence between the two was oppressive.

"I'll do whatever it takes to help, Jake," Natasha suddenly said. Jake looked over his game of pool and approached the jukebox. He got close, reached past her, and tapped on the glass at a track.

"All I need is a copy," he said.

"Okay," she agreed. She made the selection for him. She watched him walk. He was confident but unsteady, not quite on the right path even in a short distance.

Outside, Harvey pulled up in his cop car in response to the unexpectedly loud sounds of Jake's Mustang. He noticed Natasha's car was parked alongside it. Foregoing all police procedures or protocol, he took out his phone and made a short recording.

Just three seconds. All he needed.

Inside, Jake poured himself a beer into a frosted glass and moved to skull it all down before the fast driving rock song ended, but Natasha stopped him.

"You don't need this," she said. She gently took the beer away and propped it up on the flat back of the jukebox. A new song started, a slower and more composed arena rock ballad. Jake eyed his beer fondly until Natasha moved in his way and started to sway with him. He swayed back, and before he knew it, they were dancing—lightly shifting side to side.

Natasha looked up to see how he was feeling. His days had been long, and he looked tired, sad, and vulnerable at the end of it all. Like he didn't know what drastic disappointment would hit him next. Like an amateur who just woke up from his first blackout and couldn't tell if the one over him was the ref waking him up or the man trying to kill him for glory.

"I miss you," she whispered, wondering if he heard. He did and put his hands upon her shoulders. His big, callused hands rested on her firm yet drooping shoulders as she pressed into him. He felt her coming on, but he just couldn't get in the mood. Reminders of an unforgiven failure surrounded him. Not in his own mother's home and bar.

"Ma always told me," he admitted, "I was a fool for leaving you."

"Your mum knew what she was talking about," she said with a smirk. He leaned down and hugged her and let his face rest on her shoulder. "The part you protect," she went on, "the part you try to kill is the part I've always loved."

Jake sighed into her blouse. The drink was finally dragging him down hard. "Please," he spoke and struggled to conclude for a moment, "stay with me tonight."

Natasha let his question hang for just a second. "Okay."

Jake looked up and prepared to rise and meet her eye to eye, but something caught his attention. Way in the back, past the bar, he thought he saw someone moving through the staff-only area that led to the upstairs. In fact, he knew he did. He gently pushed himself away and walked to the back of the room.

"Wait here for a minute," he said.

"Where are you going?"

Jake clenched his fist in front of his chest, tight and hard, to get pumped up. "Pee."

Jake hiked up the stairs in a storm at first, then quieted his approach and took on an element of stealth. He saw a lamp light on in his mother's room and slowly crept up to inspect around the corner. Someone was in there. They'd moved the bed and the carpet aside and were in the black bags. They opened up the tin and pocketed the discarded mobile phone, then shoved everything back and turned to leave.

Jake blocked the way. "What are you doing?" he insisted. He stared down his brother AJ, who was dressed all in dark clothing. It wasn't the reunion he planned on having once his brother got away from their pursuers.

"We're getting the fuck out of here, Jake," AJ insisted.

"Now?" Jake asked.

"Yeah, now," AJ said. He looked over Jake's shoulder in a panic. "What the hell you doing with a cop? You want me killed?"

"It's Natasha," Jake said.

AJ shook his head. "She's a copper now."

"And she can help us," Jake insisted, blowing a stiff and very alcohol-fueled breath into AJ's face.

"I don't trust her," AJ said emphatically. "I don't trust no one in this town. No, Jake, you can be a sitting duck. Cause they will come, and she can't do a thing about it to protect you. I'm taking this," he held up the phone from his pocket, "I'm going to dads, and then I'm leaving."

"Jake!" Natasha called from downstairs. "Are you okay?"

Jake stood against AJ. He was bigger, but he was far drunker. AJ was smaller but wide awake, agile, and in full control of himself. They were both determined to act, but neither found the room to move...

Chapter 23

Harvey sat outside the pub for some time and lit up a cigarette. He'd gotten what he wanted and lingered for a while longer, hoping Natasha would come out soon. When she didn't, the lights downstairs and upstairs went off; he departed for the station.

As he did, he missed a vagrant traveling by way of a side road out that led out of town towards the club. A single man on a motorbike—a Kawasaki no less—pushed his vehicle up the long road with a black bag balanced over the handlebars.

AJ was on his own for the time being. He entered town so that he could get a clean break with no one looking and get away. There was only one person left he could trust, and they were already far out on the road, but not so far he couldn't find them again. Once he was clear of the town, away from all forms of prying eyes and ears, he kicked the throttle on and rode out. Things leveled out for him and his extra cargo as he went on the long, smooth road.

The night ended, and the morning brought a hazy brightness to Jake's hungover eyes. After a short but deep sleep, he awoke in his mother's bed at the crack of dawn and forced himself to push through the pounding headache with practiced measures. He got a shower that started cold and ended hot, then went to the kitchen behind the bar to cook up a pot of coffee. While he did, he took a large soup pot and filled it with water. He left that outside where Max waited. The big dog dipped his whole face in and started lapping up water, simultaneously splashing the front porch clean.

Jake poured two cups of coffee, one for himself and one to help rouse Natasha from her place. She'd chosen the pool table as an impromptu bed. She woke up to see Jake standing over her. The hangover didn't hit her as hard, but she was still bleary-eyed and groggy like she'd already started drinking to nurse the headache down.

"What time is it?" she moaned.

"Ten," Jake said. Natasha checked over his shoulder to confirm. It was about ten-til ten, but ten enough. Seeing the time woke her straight up again, and she hopped down to the floor.

"I must get going," she said, "to see mum before I start work." Jake held out her share of coffee to the open air as she ran out of the pub to her car. He heard her start the engine before he even got to the window and just caught her pull away when he looked outside.

Natasha whipped herself back into shape for the rest of the day and got to work just on time for her late-morning shift to start. She had work to do in two ways. Her regular official duties came first, but between those, she had her own concerns. She sifted through the stacks of files, all the physical forms from before and after digitization for the intermittent crime that Silver City managed to keep. Nearly all of them started or ended at the pub or were accidents on one of the two main roads. There was plenty to look through in the C cabinet alone—but none for Cambell.

No Cambell report for a death that led to a wanted poster—it didn't make sense. She was baffled. Before she could so much as whisper the question on her mind, she was interrupted from behind.

"Good morning, darling," Harvey said. She turned with a start, just quick enough to see Harvey's sinister grin soften a little into something more seductive and leering. He was a lot closer than he sounded as well. She had to put her hand on her chest to keep her heart from beating out of it.

"God, Harvey!" she exclaimed. She closed the folder behind her back and put it back in the cabinet.

"Started to worry," he said. "You weren't answering my calls."

She paused. She could sense the suspicion in his voice. "I had my phone off for a bit."

Harvey closed in on her. She stood her ground, but in her mind, she felt like dodging out of the way with the way he skulked at her. "Looks like you've hardly slept," he said, lightly taking her chin in a pinching grip to turn her face side to side. "Did your mother have you....running around again?"

She sighed and took offense to his tone. "Why call me after work?"

Harvey got aggressive and formal. He started talking down to her as a superior on the force. "It's a twenty-four-seven job we got finding this bloke-"

"My mother didn't have me running around-"

"I need you to be available-"

Natasha waved her hands and parted the air to end the constant interruptions of talking over one another. "I'll keep my phone on next time."

Harvey leaned against the wall and seemed to shift tone immediately. "How is mum?"

She sighed. "She's drowsy from the medication. Her doctor says it will be some time until she can walk again. Until then, I help" Natasha redirected herself away from his distraction. "...why? Why exactly did you call?"

"Don't want to get our hopes up, but there was a sighting of AJ yesterday—turned out not to be him. So be a good thing you have your phone on at all times." Natasha nodded understandingly. "Do you have time for dinner sometime this week?"

Natasha looked up at him blankly and then past him before she had to react to his invitation with appropriate disgust. There was a mother entering the station with two children at her side. "What? Ah, no, Harvey. Let's keep this professional from now on...." She gauged his reaction. His face was blank, official, on the clock. "I have to see to these people."

She walked past him to greet and deal with the entrants, leaving Harvey in the room. He checked that her back was turned to him and inspected the cabinet folder for what she was sifting through. The C files were just a bit out of place.

Chapter 24

AJ was out of town but not out of trouble. His green Kawasaki rumbled down the road and took every nasty bump in the sun-cracked asphalt with a shudder. He rumbled across the landscape and took a sharp left onto a dirt road that led into a thick field of scrub.

Far behind, out of earshot and beyond a film of roadside dust, two more bikers followed him. They saw where he turned and slowed down as they approached the same turn. One went forward slightly just to check and threw a thumbs up to the rider behind him. They followed the shallow tracks AJ's lightweight bike made. While one biker went ahead, the other stopped in the road and made a call on an old flip phone.

AJ was up ahead. He navigated through the brush and snaked his way off the main road. The dust from his bike left a red film on the already reddish plants he sped past. He had his hand on the throttle and gave it a quick jerk when he saw a bump in the way. He ramped over stones and idled his way through the smoother undergrowth.

His engine started to sputter. Every jerk forward felt like a desperate push instead of a smooth roll. He cranked the throttle again. The sound was no longer a satisfying thundery growl but a whiny shriek. He heard a cough and felt the involuntary jerk take over beneath him.

The sound of his bike died out just as he emerged from the thick hedge to the outskirts of a town. Far enough from Silver City, but still part of its local area code. The same environment connected by dual-lane roads and a lifeless expanse that either town shared ownership of. He didn't even know the name of the place, but he knew well enough to roll between some buildings to keep himself hidden.

He coasted across the gap between the edge of town and the bush and got halfway. He shifted into neutral and started pushing to keep himself moving until he reached the pavement at the rear of a building. It was a good enough place to keep his bike hidden. He moved it behind a big green dumpster bin behind an abandoned building and hoisted the bags over his shoulders.

He jogged out into the ghost town. Every storefront and house in the distance looked abandoned. The roads were in a state of disrepair so bad that gaps opened into the sewers below between the asphalt and the concrete pavement. Every window was either covered with dust or cracked.

He jogged across the town, through alleys and avoiding all the streets he could. He heard a rare sound of high revving engines in the distance as someone passed through. It wasn't a town full of places to stop. Not for ordinary people, but it was for him.

The car that came into town was an unmarked white van, with rusty red around the tire rims and a haze of brown around the skirting. A man stepped out, tall and wide with an imposing face, and looked around. A young couple with a stroller saw him on the sidewalk and turned to walk away. The few people left in town were out and about in the only avenue where businesses could live.

Tony stood beside the white van and inspected the surroundings. He saw some of his boys moving in and out of the local shops, leaving the clerks inside confused or off-put. He got another call and snapped his phone open with a quick flick.

AJ made his way across town to the outskirts on the other side, mostly unseen, and arrived at a graveyard. It was the one place that was, unfortunately, the most familiar to him. The graveyard shared the same space as Silver City. It laid between them in the open expanse, a lone plot of sadness in the middle of the baked land.

He walked through the field of stones to one, in particular, inconspicuously placed off to the side in the middle of a longer row. The tombstone had no shade or cover and was one of the newer postings in the ground.

Kelly Cambell. Born 1956—Died 2014—Age 59

His own mother's tombstone had no kind parting words or epitaph, just the facts. Facts that made AJ's hands shake. He knelt and tried to talk candidly to her through the ground.

"I'll be out of here, and I'll come back and visit...You had my back always. That I'll never forget. Love you, Ma."

AJ held his stance low to the ground and let his hand linger on the dirt below the stone. He stood up with a sigh and took out his phone. He scrolled down to the contact listed as *DAD* and paused before he pressed the button.

As he made his call, another one ended. At the edge of the scrubs, the bikers followed the trail through to the edge of town and found AJ's bike leaned up against the alley. The biker leaned down and tested the engine with a quick touch. Still hot, just parked. They were just barely behind him. The one who received that information snapped his phone shut and shoved it into his pocket.

Tony signaled his men to board up into the van. They were hot on the trail, one that led out into the badlands and farther away from town than before. AJ made his way out of town, with a dusty trail of shallow footprints, through the scrubs and the forests and back out to the flat pan of the salt lake. It was flat and wide open before him, nothing on any side to protect him.

He left some of his family behind and headed towards the family he still had left. Someone who could understand him and help without questions.

Chapter 25

Harvey returned to the pub in the day. Even when it was open and staffed, he knew that the hours weren't kind to daytime drinkers or even wandering tourists. If it was before noon, the previous owner was either asleep or just not ready to move around yet. The new owner, or landholder, was far worse.

He tested the door. The chime overhead jingled in a slight breeze as Harvey tried his best to yank the door off its lock. He tried it multiple times out of anger until his constant shunting provoked Max.

Harvey turned to the growling dog. He was a length away and bound by a chain onto one of the posts, not quite guarding the door so much as acting as an alarm. He also noticed the chime overhead, ringing in the wind. He also noticed the keyring hidden just barely in sight over the bell, wedged between the wood and the metal plate.

He took it off and looked over the key. He memorized the address and put it back. Max continued to growl even as Harvey turned to leave, so he stopped and turned back. "Woof! Woof!" Harvey taunted Max with false barks and provoked the big dog into replying with a few growling barks that jerked him forward on his chain. Harvey smirked as he headed back to his car and returned to the station.

Harvey's hands were white-knuckled to the wheel. He went at a moderate pace, all according to the law, but still pushed his car hard on the straightaways and broke hard around free corners. The sounds of his tires and engine were muffled under the sound of his favored music. His head rocked and tilted in tune and harmony with the rising Italian arias that he listened to.

He arrived at the station and pulled into his designated spot. As he got out, he felt something was amiss and looked to the station. Somehow, beyond the doors and walls, he felt like something was off. His instincts kicked in, and he rushed for the door.

Inside, Natasha was at his desk. She couldn't find any reports on the Cambell case. It was like they buried the files with the body. Nothing remained, not even of the manuscript for the wanted poster, something they could only produce with an excess of careful legal petitioning. She couldn't find anything in paper, and the online reporting was still months behind.

She heard a bell chime from the front as someone entered. She shot up and shut everything she opened at the same time that the door closed. She ducked around the corner, out of sight from over the reception desk, and got to the coffee station. She filled a dirty mug with thin coffee still too fresh to be considered real coffee at all and stood at attention as Harvey rounded the corner.

"I'll have one while you're at it," he said. She turned and

saw him wander in with a bagged lunch in one hand. He sat behind his desk without a second thought and leaned back in his seat. She looked over, carefully, to see if anything else was amiss, any drawers she left cracked open or papers out of place, but there was nothing. What she did see, as he ate aggressively, was a ring of keys around his belt.

"Oh," he said, as he wiped his mouth and swallowed his roll, "you know what?"

Natasha stared ahead, stiff, waiting for him to continue so she wouldn't have to give herself cover. She felt a sudden heat over her hand, a steaming sensation that reminded her mug was full.

"Shit," she exclaimed.

"What you say?" he asked.

Natasha sucked on her burnt index finger and blew on it to try and cool it off. "Oh, I just made a mess," she explained. "What?" Harvey rocked forward in his seat, and the keys jingled briefly. Natasha kept her eyes on them while his eyes turned away. She reached back for the mug and gripped it by the handle, and tipped it to pour just a little bit more out from the overflowed rim.

"We are this close," he said, pinching the air, "to capturing that murderer."

"Oh really?" Natasha said. She took a deep, quick breath to regain her composure. She walked over with the mug and held it out to the side, far enough that Harvey couldn't see how full it was while he looked at her.

"Turns out," Harvey said, with a sly stroke of his mustache, "that Brother of his been protecting him."

Natasha carefully passed the mug over, broadside to him, and leaned forward. She waited until the rim was over his lap before his hand met it and shook it with a quick spin of her wrist. A bit of the hot water splashed out and into his hand, which made him jerk it in a slapping motion. It missed the mug, but she used the opportunity to let go—as if he hit it himself— and the rest spilled onto his leg.

"I'm so sorry!" she exclaimed.

Harvey shot up in a panic and stood for just a second to assess his situation before the burning sensation hit him through his pants.

"Ah shit, hell!" he exclaimed in a flustered, growling whisper. Natasha reached for a cup of plain water and made sure it was on her side of his desk, out of his reach.

"Take your pants off!" she said. Harvey, still in a slight panic, cocked his eyebrow at her suggestion, but the pain kept him from being too leering for long. He winced, and his hands tensed into fists. Natasha bent down and undid his belt and zipper for him.

"Hell," Harvey said, "just as well I keep spares."

"Go put them on now," she said as she pulled his pants to his ankles. He stepped out of his shoes and patted down his reddened thigh. "I'll wash these now."

Harvey left the room in a bemused hurry, leaving Natasha to wash off and de-stain his pants. As soon as he was gone,

Natasha took the keys off the ring and started opening the drawers she couldn't access before, starting with the one on the bottom left. She tried keys as fast as possible until one fit but wouldn't twist. She another—it fit, turned, and creaked the lock open.

Inside was what looked like the interior of an evidence locker. A solid block of cocaine was bundled up and walled in with stacks of cash. Underneath it, all was a folder, and she suspected it was what she was looking for. She picked it up and placed it on the floor so it stayed out of sight in case Harvey came back too soon.

Police Report Case Number: 07854100 Date—13 August 2014. The date of the accident and the death of Jake's mom. She took out her phone and took pictures, one by one, of each page at the highest fidelity she possibly could. She finished, placed the papers back, and slipped it back under the cocaine brick and money. She gave the whole dirty drawer a sneer before she closed and locked it back up.

Harvey returned to see Natasha leaning over his pants on the floor, rubbing on the leg with a crumpled-up napkin. "Good as new," he said. "Need a hand?"

Natasha stood up with his pants and tried to unclip his belt, but the keyring prevented her from properly feeding it through the loops. Harvey took it from her and assisted by unclipping the keys, then let her do the rest of the work.

"Hey, I was thinking," she began, "I'll take you on your offer for dinner."

Harvey blinked in surprise. "Why the sudden change?" She

handed him his belt, and he looped it around in a single, quick motion.

"Oh well," she began, with a more sultry sort of tone, "that little accident back there...brought back some fond memories...." She playfully bit her lip and smiled at him. "I'll be taking these home to wash."

She turned to leave, but Harvey took her by the wrist. Her heart skipped a beat in fear. She looked down as he turned her around to check the drawer, to see if she left anything out of line or noticeable. Then her eyes wandered up to his, which were full of lusty expectation.

"When?" he asked.

"When what?"

"Dinner?"

She nodded, mouth open, and forced herself to curl a smile. "Surprise me." She left with his wet pants draped over her arm and her cell phone, heavy with incrimination, in her pocket.

Chapter 26

J ake was up in the afternoon and headed out. He took a different route out of town, past the through-lane business row and over the empty expanse toward the old town. He was drawn there over a passing memory. AJ's presence spurred him to visit the grave, something he hadn't done since the burial, what felt like weeks ago.

He slowly rolled his way through town and noticed the thugs of Tony's gang were out and about in the streets. They walked out of shops, no doubt leaving the customers inside terrified and crowded around a white van. Jake stayed a block away and slowly rolled across the way to see what he could out of the side of his Mustang without getting spotted.

He saw Tony barking orders into a cell phone while his free hand wrangled up and commanded his boys that couldn't speak English. They all followed his directions, like a conductor waving a baton for gruesome animals in biker leather.

Jake felt hot and shaken. The shaking originated from his phone, but the heat was further down. He knew the man across the way. The foul-mouthed nefarious gangster was responsible for something. No accidents could happen with a man like that around.

He answered his phone to stop the buzzing and talked with his eyes fixed on the action far off.

"Jake!" Mike greeted. "It's Mike from Reggie's Real Estate. How are you today?"

"Fine, Mike," Jake monotonously answered.

"Great to hear," Mike said, not picking up the impatience in Jake's voice. "The owners of the building are flying in tomorrow morning for an inspection. Eleven O'clock works for you?"

Jake watched as Tony boarded the van. A second later, it rolled down the street to scoop up the other members.

"Perfect," Jake said. The white van sped up the street in his direction. He pulled forward down the road and stopped in an alley. His eyes shifted to his rearview, and he waited for the van to flash by.

"Have it spick and span, won't you?" Mike said.

"Okay, thanks, Mike," Jake said. "See you tomorrow." He hung up just as he saw and heard the van trundle past. He put his car in reverse and sped out into the street. He did a blind J-turn and righted himself to pursue the van from behind.

He was in hot pursuit—too hot. He could hear the roar of his engine as he prepared to shift up into a faster gear. Just as his revs maxed, he saw someone about to cross the street, a mother pushing a stroller. Jake slammed on the brake and squealed to a stop as the van pulled away up the next street.

"Are you fucking crazy!?" The mother snapped. She pulled

her stroller back and walked up to the passenger side of Jake's car. She looked furious—raging, even. Jake looked ahead. The white van took a left-hand turn. He peeled away from the mother as she screamed at him, "You fucking lunatic!" and flipped the bird at his mirrors.

He chased them down out of town. It was just them on the road. Jake stayed safely away but couldn't help slowly catching up. His car was faster, stronger, and solidly better in all respects. It wasn't hard to get caught up, but he knew he had to stay safely away.

His chase was cut short. A bright red light met his eyes just above his wheel on the dashboard. His fuel warning light. He glanced up just as he passed the petrol station at the edge of town. The van was ahead of him and showed no signs of slowing on the long road out of town toward the salt flats. Jake huffed angrily and smacked his steering wheel.

He slowed to a stop, reversed, and turned to go back up the road. No swinging drifting U-turn for him. He just needed to get back toward town. His pursuit could wait. It couldn't, but it had to.

Jake splashed his tank as fast as he could and tried to scan his card to pay for it, but the already antiquated reader was off. No warning sign. The whole mechanism was just dark and shut down. He stomped into the station to pay and noticed, besides the same bullshit poster of his brother, the clerk inside looked panicked and was reaching for the phone. Jake put his hands up to show he was no threat.

The clerk pointed to the picture. Then, with a tense face and wide eyes, he pointed to the back room. Jake looked between them, then met the clerk's eyes with a steely expression. He moved his hand down slowly—for him to put the phone down. The clerk stood, confused. Jake flared at him and made a more stern motion to press the phone down with enough force to break it. The clerk met him halfway and hung up before he finished dialing.

Jake moved silently to the door and turned to the attendant to get back. Jake reached for the handle and slowly turned it until it hit a limit. It was locked from the other side. Jake stepped back, glanced at the attendant in the corner, then did a spinning snap kick to the door like he was trying to break a jaw. He snapped the door off its lock, and the whole thing swung in with tremendous force.

A man on the other side fell over onto his back. Jake leaped forward and seized him on the ground, ready to start hammering the man's face against the mat. He was in a sudden fight mode. He barely noticed that it was AJ underneath him until he was already in a prime submission position.

Jake stopped himself short and waited for AJ to open his eyes. Once AJ saw who came for him, he went through a rapidly paced series of shock, surprise, relief, and exhilaration. Jake pulled him up to his feet by his collar and stabilized him on his soles.

"Let's get out of here," Jake said. He ran out, with AJ following close behind. The clerk was left speechless and unsure of what to do. Jake jumped into the driver's seat, and AJ quickly stepped around with an armful of baggage and threw himself into the passenger side. Jake peeled out the moment his brother was in.

The clerk saw it all happen as they fled down the road and picked up the phone. He wasn't sure whether to call about the bounty he spotted or about the gas-dasher. Either way, he didn't know what to say. He didn't get the license plate, and they'd be long gone before the cops ever arrived....

Chapter 27

All was calm at the police station. Harvey sat at his desk and looked over a key tag which he slipped into his shirt pocket. He turned the silver frame over and rocked his head from side to side, enjoying a piece of music from his memory.

Natasha entered and distracted him with her apparel. She was dressed in sporty gym clothes and had a duffle bag at her side, from which she took out Harvey's freshly cleaned pants. "Why, thank you," Harvey said. She handed them over across the table and spotted the photograph of them on the corner of his desk.

"Wow," she said, trying to mask her uncomfortableness. "You still have a photo of us together?"

"In my mind," he said, "we never broke up."

She smiled at him, trying to take his remark as a compliment. "Okay. Bye."

She turned and sauntered out. Harvey gazed at her rear as she went, which she unintentionally shifted about in a way that pleased him. Once she was out of sight, his eyes drifted over to the photo. All of a sudden, the phone rang. It shook Harvey out of his comfortable position. He stomped his boots on the ground and raced to pick it up.

But it was already too late. The call came minutes, and therefore miles after Jake and AJ were away. The black mustang moved like the shadow of a cloud across the tarmac. Jake kept them steady on the road without a solid plan. Meanwhile, AJ cracked open the tin jerry can and took out a wallet filled with cards.

"What're you doing?" Jake asked.

"Mud map," AJ said. He handed Jake a folded-up photograph of a map drawn in the dirt. He waited while Jake studied it. Jake looked at him with a curious, almost accusing eye. "You can't miss it," AJ instructed. "A stand-alone white pad just off Old Palm road."

"I won't be dropping by," Jake said. AJ could tell there was still tension between them from the night before and the endless questions that Jake was left with. Still, a barrier of mistrust, and AJ knew his word alone wasn't enough to break it down. AJ took the tin and placed it on the spacious dashboard. He took out another photo of a baby in a pink onesie.

"Who's that?" Jake asked.

AJ held it up with a proud, kind of sad smile. "My baby girl Casey," he said. He became glum. "She'd be three by now."

"A daughter?" Jake said. "I didn't know that." He passed the photo over. Jake held it in one hand and steadied the wheel with the other. Jake glanced at it. She looked happy, a rarity in all the baby pictures he remembered being in. He handed it back.

"Why would you?" AJ said as he took the photo back.

"Mum would be the first to tell me over the phone," Jake said.

"I never told her," AJ admitted. He let silence fill the car as his thoughts caught up with him. "Eventually, I was going to. That was the plan. For us to leave, head up North and meet her Granddaughter. That will never be." His eyes teared up. "Why is that our Family—us! Has never really been around for each other. Mum did her fuckin best! And now she's dead!"

"That's because Dad was never there!" Jake exclaimed. "Ok! He left! He fucked off! He destroyed what we had as a Family. The shit that he put mum through! You, me!" Jake's anger snuffed out the conversation. AJ was in no state to stand against it. It bowled him over—the rage was too much for AJ to even agree with. Jake turned forward and let himself cool down. "I'll make sure you go back and be with your Daughter," he promised.

AJ didn't reply. He looked forward and inspected the terrain. They were heading toward the salt flats and the old town. "My bike is close," AJ said. "Let me out here." Jake slowed the car down and pulled over to the gravely shoulder. The car rocked to a stop and left the brothers in another awkward pause, broken up by the idling growls of the engine in park.

"Look," AJ began, "I know you're just as angry at the old man as I am for leaving and being a fucked up drunk. I mean, look at us. We're doing the same shit! We need to fight for change in one another. He's our dad. And he's sick."

"Yeah, sick all right," Jake grumbled.

"Nah," AJ said. "I mean sick-sick—as in dying sick." Jake

looked at him with disbelief and alert. "You saw him? He didn't tell you?"

"No," Jake uttered.

AJ looked his brother in the eyes and hesitated a bit to see how brutal his truth should be. But with Jake, he figured that he'd been through more brutal beatings in his life. "The old man's got Cancer, Jake. The least we can do is visit him before we leave. He's our Dad."

Jake just stared along dead-eyed, mouth slack. He sat back in his seat for a moment to take the news in. Eventually, AJ got out, and Jake followed. They embraced and patted each other on the back.

"I'm going to get the money," AJ said. Jake pulled away and watched AJ make his way bravely, sure-footedly into the terrain of the outback. He turned and called back, "I'm going straight to dad's—we split this and get the fuck out!" Jake watched AJ head out for a moment and contemplated what to do next. What he even could do.

He heard a buzzing sound inside his car and rushed to take care of it. To his shock, it was just his phone on the dashboard. He picked it up and read the message.

I'm at the pub with the report.

Only one person could have sent it. He replied: *Coming now!* as fast as his fingers could type. He tossed it onto the passenger seat, hit first gear, slammed the accelerator, and spun around in the road to head back into town again.

AJ looked back at the cloud of dust the Mustang billowed

up as the sound of his brother's engine faded away. He soldiered forward regardless and made his way to the rear of town again. His bike was still behind the dumpster, still hidden green against green from any streetside suspicion.

He filled up the petrol from the can he brought with him and mounted up to kick it into gear. He thrust his foot down on the starter, but nothing. He tried again and listened closely to what the problem was. The starter wasn't even kicking over, just empty thudding under the seat. He stepped off and leaned down over the bike to inspect it.

One of the spark plugs was missing. All that remained was a snapped lead. He was shocked. He stood up just as he heard the screech of tires as a white van pulled in at the end of the alley. AJ was confused. He turned to the sound of a whoosh through the air as a steel pipe hit him in the back of the head.

Everything went dark. He fell, and his photos scattered out of his pocket onto the alleyway.

Chapter 28

Jake didn't get back until evening. He didn't hear back from AJ all the time and kept his hand close to his pocket in case his phone buzzed. When he did return, he saw Natasha's car out in front of the pub. He passed by and saw her waiting in the driver's seat.

Jake wrapped around the block and parked his Mustang at the bar's back entrance, the space reserved for the owner, usually blocked up by Sara, but he took it and worked his way around the pub. Max was on full alert at the rumble of the Mustang's engine and the complimentary purr of Natasha's car.

The door was open for him. He slid in, and they were off as soon as he got the door closed. Natasha had them on the move for some reason, and he didn't question why. Eyes on the pub, perhaps. She also wasn't in her standard cop car or uniform. She was working off the beat to get him in the loop.

He read through the reports on her mobile phone, all the seedy details of the accident that were left out, along with the inclusion of drug busts and missing money—the black bags— all pinned on AJ as if it was an afterthought. The shoddiest police reporting he'd ever seen. Jake had walked through back-office verbal beatdowns for drunken slip-ups and sponsorship contract breaches that were more carefully put together overnight.

He stopped at one of the collected photos in the report of the helpful bloke with the white Ute. Natasha pulled over and turned off the engine. They were out of town, still in sight of the last few lights across Silver City's darkened skyline.

"You know him?" she asked.

"We caught up yesterday," he said.

"And?"

"Gavin Fletcher," Jake said. "He said nothing about being a witness or making a statement, said he was out of town working in the mines when he heard news of it."

Natasha looked confused. "Why would someone make a false statement as a witness?"

"Because someone's paying," Jake said. He leaned back in the seat to think. Natasha looked at him intensely. He reached an epiphany. "Of course. He would've alerted your Station yesterday. Out of nowhere, the gang knew where we were. Which would mean someone at your Station is working close to the gang. The other cop that works with you?"

"Charlie?" she said.

"Did he happen to be at the scene?" Jake asked.

Natasha reviewed the incident as she remembered it for a moment in her head. "No. He told me about it the next morning. He said he stayed back to mind the station."

"Maybe fish for some information," Jake suggested. "Ask Charlie did he see Gavin make the statement that night back at the station? Did he read the report?"

"Okay," she said. "He's working tonight."

"But be careful...." Jake said. "I think the best thing is to have the city police come in to have Gavin investigated once we can generate some proof. Don't want Harvey catching on that we are on to him." She nodded limply. Jake reached across the car's center console, held himself up on the handbrake, and leaned in to kiss Natasha quickly before he exited the car. It left her stunned, but she recovered once she saw him standing out of the door.

"Where are you going?" she called.

"I will pick you up tomorrow," Jake said, "at noon."

"Don't you want me to drop you off at the pub?" she asked.

He shook his head. "I don't want anyone to see you with me," he said. He shut the door and started to jog off like it was just part of his nightly routine. Natasha checked him in her rearview as he flickered between the distant streetlights that led into town. She nodded her head in the mirror to psyche herself up. A dire investigation was underway.

Corruption that settled in under her own feet and festered at the apparatus of justice she defended. It made her feel a certain sensation fill her, like a flood of water—a warm rage lifted in her and propelled her forward.

Little did either know, but the case deepened drastically. While Jake ran to settle his affairs and get in contact with AJ, his brother was already apprehended and taken to the clubhouse. The gang found him and were prepared to make an example of him. They fashioned a cross out of railway sleepers and tied him to it. His face was blood-soaked, and his body was limp. He breathed in wheezes with his bruised stomach, as his ribs were too beaten to push in and out.

Tony paced around in front of his torture subject while the members all hung back, acting as gophers and bag boys for the miscreant master's bag of tricks. Behind him was another member, an uncommon face among the rabble, but one that harnessed equal respect from the men and equal fear from AJ. Harvey donned the member attire, foregoing his policeman's uniform, and blended in like a natural. Without his cop trappings, he looked like he belonged there easily.

Tony shined a bright hand torch into AJ's face. The light forced AJ's eyes to squint, and all the muscles in his face contracted painfully. "We checked all over," Tony said, "no cash to be found there. The kid at the station says a bloke in a black Mustang came and picked him up."

Harvey stepped forward to the side of the light as an imposing shadow in AJ's path. "You gave the cash to your brother?"

AJ could barely speak, so he made his words count with the hardest truth he could deliver. "He's not involved," he weakly insisted. Harvey didn't listen and gave him a stiff uppercut to his torso. It stopped AJ from breathing for a few seconds.

"Did you put it in the boot of his car?" Harvey asked. "Be a good place, yes?"

"He's not involved," AJ demanded.

"Too late for that," Harvey said. "He is now." He reached into his pocket and dangled a set of keys in front of AJ's face that glinted off of the bright light. "The only way to a man's heart is to go through his family." Harvey turned and tossed the keys over to Tony.

AJ took in a sharp breath through a wall of clotted blood and snot. "Good luck finding where he lives," AJ said.

"I don't need luck," Harvey said. "I've got the eyes of the town." Harvey took Tony's torch and rammed the hot, exposed glass hard into AJ's stomach. His practice with police batons made it hurt especially bad. AJ managed to summon up a howl of pain from deep in his tortured guts.

"Untie him!" Harvey hollered. "Get him down!" The men scrambled to follow his commands while the rest got ready to move out. Two unlocked and pushed the gates in front of the white van. All AJ could do was listen as he heard the gang move out in a roar of engines that created thunder across the plains. He knew where they were going, at least in part, and couldn't do anything but suffer on the floor and hope.

Hope his brother could handle them in a way he couldn't. That his rage could somehow find power in Jake's fists....

Chapter 29

Natasha pulled up to the police station and found it unexpectedly dark. Uneventful as things were, the need for police coverage across all hours was highlighted with the presence of the gangs. Even if they couldn't do much, being seen as present by the town was a better morale boost than simply locking up the doors and hiding at home. But the sight of the station in darkness had the opposite effect.

It served her purpose better, though. She couldn't ask Charlie, but she knew deep down it probably wasn't an option in the first place. He was easier to work with than Harvey, who was definitely on some kind of bad take, but she couldn't trust him with the truth. She knew Charlie was closer to Harvey than he was to the law.

She crept in and went straight to Harvey's office, where she noticed a dim, flickering light. She opened the door to a bizarrely overdressed office. Rose petals, silky sheets, candlelight, and a pleasant scent filled the air.

"Charlie?" she whispered. No response. She passed by Harvey's decorated desk and went for Charlie's first. His wasn't as well decorated, just covered with normal papers. She checked Harvey's set up as she passed by and read a note settled underneath a lazy wreath of white roses.

Hello sweetness

I trust you're here now. I won't be long.

Getting a few celebration drinks for Dinner

Harvey xx

She ignored the letter and searched the room for something new, some sign that a report or some evidence was moved around more than yesterday. She could hear her heart racing inside her chest, not at all helped by the creepy assertion of the letter.

"Hello," she heard. A dark and gritty voice she recognized easily. It caused her to jump. She jerked around and saw a silhouette casually leaning against the wall next to the door. The candlelight flickered intermittently as if it was avoiding illuminating him. She could barely see a smirk on his face and a glint off the glass bottle in his hand. He helped it up to show it off in better light. Champagne, still wrapped and corked.

"No need to be startled, darling," he said. He gripped the neck of the bottle hard, undid the wrapper, and popped the cork halfway across the room. Natasha chuckled weakly as the fizz of the drink broke the eerie silence between them.

"Where's Charlie?" she asked.

"Charlie's been working like a dog of late," he said. "He deserved a night off."

"What's the occasion?' she asked, pointing to his bottle.

He held it up expectantly. "Dinner."

Natasha's unexpected hold-up was nothing compared to what was happening across town. Jake returned from his fake jog and made his way through the recently re-learned streets toward the pub. He ran under the streetlights and avoided the light from the few windows that still stayed on in the evening. What was curious was one light in particular that stood out from the rest, right around the back of the pub.

He heard Max going wild as well. The strong dog was barking up a storm in the middle of town. Jake broke out into a run to confront the dog and see what was troubling him. Max was a guard dog. He only made that kind of noise to strangers but was trained not to bother people going in and out of the front door.

Jake stopped short to get Max untied. The big dog was yanking at his collar tight enough to nearly break it already. All his wild rage was aimed at the back of the house, at the mysteriously bright glow. It was too bright and too inconsistent to be a street lamp. And besides that, Jake knew there was no street lamp back there. Just the garage.

And his car.

The thought loosened Jake's grip, and Max went bolting around the side of the house. Jake followed and was stopped as the light grew bright enough to smack him like he'd just recovered his vision after a staggering head-side blow, and the first thing he saw was stadium lights. It was bright, orange, and burning hot. Like he opened up an oven to something on fire.

His Mustang sat in drive, covered in flames. The fire

chewed at the interior and melted the plastics against the metal frame. The fire came from the top but quickly descended as it burned its way through the car. The bonnet was alight as well. The fire cascaded down like a slick, bright waterfall.

Jake was distracted by Max. The dog was barking loud at something in the darkness. Jake could take a guess what, but the fire was closer and more of a problem. He stood shocked, utterly confused at what to do. The fire was uncontrollable. The whole Mustang was like a bowl of burning oil.

It felt like his rage was about to peak.

The fire reached the engine under the bonnet. That was the first thing to burst. The metal crumpled and dented from fragments of the engine shattering and bursting upward. The fire quickly spread and caused the exhaust in the back to belch flames as the remaining gas leaked in and caught fire as well. The embers reached up as the smoke pillar turned from black to thundery red.

"Max! Come here!" Jake shouted. The dog didn't listen and ran past the fire to the back entrance. Jake shielded his face as he ran past the car. He liked that car. It was something he could never get back, a timeless design and an import that his previous pay grade could barely afford.

He ran after Max into the alley, where he was confronted by two beaming lights and two roaring, revving engines. Bikers. Thugs. Exactly the people he wanted to take his rage out on. He didn't hide his face. He showed them what they were getting into, the face of a man released from the constraints of the ring and ready to fight with no ref and no timer.

For just a moment, they paused. Then the roar of more bikes

surrounded him from the joining alley and the street. Jake saw himself surrounded and backed up to the rear of the pub, behind the garage shed. Ahead of him, on all sides, were the white beams of light from a hoard of his enemies. Behind him was a fire. Inside of him was another light, hotter than the flames that consumed his Mustang.

Like a blazing stadium light array, low enough to feel, hot enough to scald, every bulb filled and powered with the liquid heat of rage.

Chapter 30

Tires spun. Dirt flew. There was light and noise. The night was cool, but the back of the pub was hot, with a smoldering pile of burning metal heating the alleyway at Jake's back. Jake counted eight men, two on bikes and six on boots, armed with weapons. Pipes, planks, a few chains. No knives that he could see so nothing he couldn't handle.

The first attack came from dead ahead. One of the bikers rammed into Jake and knocked him over. He braced himself as best he could. It was slow but heavy, like a tackle. He dove away at the last minute to reduce the impact and rolled safely to a stop just as the other thugs surrounded him to pummel him down.

Jake sprung up with a driving straight, lifting his whole body with his fist, right into the side of one of their jaws. They were thrown back. The gang realized, in a flash, that even as a whole, they might not stand a chance against him. But they were resolved and wild. There were still five of them against one of him.

Jake swung around, grabbed one of them by the arm, stretched it out across his chest, braced it in a bar grip with his forearm, and pressed his other arm across their neck. A flying, standing armbar. Jake puffed his chest out to the limit of what the man's elbow could take. Then he let it fold back in and snapped it out with a quick jerk to snap it.

They were two down. The other two got off their bikes and came in swinging. The gangsters all gave a war shout, with one voice turning into desperate fear and pain. Jake wasn't alone in his wild fight. Max took one of the gangsters by the leg and tore straight through their riding chaps. There was blood on the ground as the gangster felt his muscles being pierced.

The first thug to swing at Jake with a weapon wielded a heavy wooden bar, part of an old push broom with a weighted tip that had a stabbing end. He swung it down hard and missed. It was an easy dodge. He wound up too long when he reared the rod over his head like a hammer. It hit the ground with a loud clack as Jake juked in on the side. He had the full range of the thug's left half to pick from. He decided to dislocate the guy's shoulder.

Jake took a blow from behind, in the back, just under his neck. They'd swung for his head and missed. He delivered a snap jab to the staff wielder's face in response and grabbed for his wooden staff. Jake wasn't a professional weapon fighter, but he knew how bludgeons worked. He swung it hard and blew a billow of dust off the ground from chest level. The thugs stepped away and held their weapons tight.

Max was still dealing with the gangsters that he could, and all they could do was hop away and jab at him with their improvised tools. One wrong flick and the guard dog's mouth would steal their weapons like Jake's iron grip stole the staff.

Jake reset his grip and tried to wield it more professionally. Like a sword. It was light in his hands.

Four men charged in. Jake swung, wide but fast, and struck one in the head, who staggered down. His swing lost momentum as it neared the next rushing combatant, so he stepped in and changed to a thrust with all the strength in his body. He jabbed the guy with the pointed tip just above the heart, between the rib and the clavicle, a dangerous soft spot.

The other two closed in quickly. Jake gripped hard with his right hand, which was choked down, and loosened his left hand. He made a backwards billiard break and hammered his fist and the hard end of the staff into the next thug. That left him holding the staff lengthwise, end to end, which he used to jab the next guy in the face and block his weapon swing. Jake choked both hands up toward the middle and rowed it, just like forearm and wrist control training at the gym. Each twist whacked the thugs as the staff twisted in a turbine motion.

The one he hit before got up and ran at him with a cleaver. Jake stepped to the side and cracked the staff into the back of the head. They fell face first and tripped over one of the members that were recovering from the heart poke. Jake finished them off with a solid piledriving jab to the solar plexus. In a small but hard area, all that force shut his breathing down and knocked him out.

The remaining gangsters ran inside to get away from Max. Jake dropped the stick and chased after them, not even pausing as he dipped down in a lunge and petted Max on the head for his good, hard work. The gangsters scrambled to lock the door. Jake made two sprinting steps and rammed it in with his shoulder.

Max ran in through Jake's legs to the pub's backroom and cornered one of the gangsters who was trailing blood. He wanted to finish his snack off and make it into a meal, and Jake wasn't obliged to stop him. That just left three more. Two made their way into the front room and tried to assault Jake in the dark.

They were going the pro-wrestling route with an overhead chair swing. The chairs of the pub were sturdy stuff but still made of light and soft wood. It didn't work. It just made Jake's shoulders sore. He gauged their distance and direction based on the attack and lunged in to grab them.

The room was just dark enough that all he could see were shadows. He had taken a few blows already, so his body started to throb, and his vision blurred, but it was nothing. It still felt like the first round. Nothing he couldn't push through. He missed his grab but heard the shuffle of feet across the floor as one retreated and the other dove in.

Jake ducked, balanced himself, lifted one leg off the ground, and shot it out behind him. A handless donkey kick. He connected with what felt like a groin and sent a man tumbling backwards with a high-pitched shout. The other, still in front, was in prime tackling range.

Jake lunged forward, arms out, and threw them forward like the pair of shears. His scissor grab caught the outlaw as they made a leftward retreat. He grabbed hard and pivoted his body to go with their weight, going from a rugby scrum to a low-stance Judo swinging throw. It sent the thug off balance and gave Jake control, enough to pivot him into what he knew was a table stacked with chairs.

He swung the man hard and assumed that he'd either hit the edge or the corner. A loud clatter of chairs and a tumbling body told him that neither was a hit. The guy piled into the booth and collapsed forward onto the floor. The other guy, still sulking in the dark, had both hands nursing his bruised groin. Jake turned to find him, the moving shadow among the dark, which sent the broken man into a scurry for the nearest door.

The bikers were in almost full retreat. Jake stayed standing and made some swings to kick them on their way out. Max mauled one of their legs and left a nasty trail in and out of their free dripping blood. The men all piled onto their bikes, two at a time, with the least concussed, taking the handles to spin out and drive away. Jake saw the last out, and Max went barking and chomping after them until the exhaust hit his face and caused him to enter a doggy sneezing fit.

The rumble of motors receded. Jake flicked on the lights and found a seat at the end of the bar. The pain of his fighting caught up to him. His back was bruised, his knuckles were raw, his arms were shaking from the excitement. Adrenaline coursed through him. He forced himself to sit still in the silence of the room.

But something continued to thump overhead. Not him or his legs. He froze up completely and listened. He heard shuffling upstairs. In his mother's room. Definite steps in the upstairs. Jake nearly bolted to investigate, but in his brief state of relaxation, he managed to have a more strategic thought.

He crept up the stairs quietly and got to the edge of the hall to peek into the room. One of the bikers slipped away from the chaos and entered the room. The bed was pushed to the side, and the carpet was flung up, but the storage space below was empty. Jake already knew that it was AJ's doing.

He assessed that the stray burglar knew what he was looking for but not where to find it. He was lost and, since all the bikes had already left, alone. Jake walked in as the would-be robber made one last check under the dresser and the nightstand before he turned around. Jake had a swinging backhand ready and connected the moment he recognized the man's face.

The thug reeled and bounced off the wall. Jake grabbed him by the throat and pushed him into the wall like he was trying to push him all the way through. It was showy, grandstanding, a totally inefficient submission hold, but without any cameras or commentators, it worked. He had the man not just by the throat but also by the brain, with one strong thumb pressing down on the thumping aorta in the neck.

"Looking for something?" Jake asked. He squeezed an airy choke out of the thug's throat before it softened up enough for him to speak. "Who's giving you orders?"

"Go fuck yourself," he strained. Jake squeezed again, throat off when he was talking and throat on when he wanted answers.

"I want a name!" Jake demanded. "Who ordered the gang to run my mother off the road, killing her?"

"She crashed herself," he wheezed.

"Was it that cop?" Jake demanded. "Harvey?"

"Okay, okay," the man said desperately. "Let go of me so I can breathe. I'll tell ya."

Jake looked the man dead in the eyes. He saw nothing but pain and heat, the look of a man at his breaking point. Jake released his grip and let the man fall on the floor to take coughing breaths. He stepped aside to give him space. The thug reached back and pulled out a flick knife. He tried to swing it forward from a crouching position. Jake pivoted around, waited for the knife-holding arm to fully extend, then grabbed it and swung him back into the wall with a crack. The knife fell to the floor.

Jake straddled in front of the man and prepared for a horizontal takedown. His opponent was at his mercy in the corner. He unleashed a hail of practiced straights and hard rights and hooks into the man's guts. The poor guy couldn't even raise his arms to block. Jake didn't count, and after 15 hits, neither did his victim.

Jake went in for a killing blow, a real one. He grabbed the gangster under their bandana and reeled them forward to chop his arm into their throat, then slammed them back into the wall. The shake made their heads whip back and smashed extra hard against the wood, and they lost all sense of balance. Jake stood back and watched them slide to the floor.

His heartbeat turned into a ringing bell. Gong after gong, the adrenaline faded as the match was won. The battle royale had one victor, and he stood over the last threat with a sense of pride. Then, a tinge of shame and just a tiny worrying reach of regret as he knelt to check his opponent's life signs. Silence.

Jake pulled the bandana off and was shocked. He knew his

opponent. It was no blind card match. He had his suspicions but never guessed the helpful and vapid Gavin would be so deep in the gang's activity that he was part of it himself.

Chapter 31

As Jake contended and easily handled his attackers, the gang split off and found the distant hermitage of Richard on the outskirts of the old town. He lived in what could only be described as a unit, a single room in a fly-by motel that was rented out for months at a time. It was a hovel full of disorganized accessories and paraphernalia with an array of medical-adjacent uses.

Two thugs broke apart from the pack and intruded into Richard's home while it was empty. They ransacked the place much like how the thugs were supposed to tear the pub apart. There was no one to stop them, so even as a force of only two, they did a significant amount of damage. Everything was out of place and pushed aside as they looked for the bags of cash.

Eventually, they left. There was nothing to find.

That's when Richard pulled in. He noticed his lights were on in his unit after he was sure he left them off. It was suspicious, all the way up to the door, which had his spare key hanging in the tumbled lock. The one he left for Jake.

He peeked in, just barely. He could hardly move. His legs were locked up from the ride, and his back ached. An unholy sum of pains racked his body. He needed medicine to dull it, which was inside, and likely scattered on the dirty carpet already.

There was no one in sight. Just a cascade of chaos and ruin of what little was left of his life. He sighed and walked his way in, up to the fridge that was still on its normal feet against the wall. All they did was open that and threw the contents on the floor. Lucky for him, they didn't bother reaching up to search the top.

He took a biscuit tin and placed it on the kitchen bench. He unsealed it and took the pistol out to look over later. Just picking it up and putting it down put a terrible twisting strain on his wrist. He took a packet of medicine out of his pocket and went to fill an unbroken glass of water to chase it down.

While it filled up, he took out an old Nokia flip phone with a charger and plugged it into the wall. The thugs hadn't broken that, thankfully. He got his glass full of water and pistol and arranged them both at his kitchen table. He sat and went into quiet contemplation. Medicine on his left, and medicine on his right. One made of chemicals and one made of lead.

His deep thoughts were interrupted by the sound of an engine. Diesel, four-stroke, a simple but effective bike, nothing like his. Something a no-name would use and be willing to ditch to keep himself alive on the open road.

Richard picked up the gun and armed it. He was weak, hurt, and afraid but not a wimp, not the kind of man who would submit to death so easily. The front door was already limply open. Someone didn't finish the job of closing it, so he'd finish them off the second they did.

The door creaked open cautiously. A figure stood in the doorway and darted out of sight just before Richard could squeeze his stalled finger against the trigger.

"It's me, Jake!" the figure called out. Richard lowered his gun in shock. Jake peeked around the corner and slowly entered with his arms up. The old man felt all the adrenaline drain from him like the bottom of a bottle fell out and took all the liquid with it. He sighed and sank back into the kitchen chair, where he coughed and slumped over with haggard breathing. "You okay?" Jake asked. He looked around the room, checked the corners high and low for signs of any stilled movement or extra bodies.

"I wasn't here," Richard said. He looked up and noticed the blood on Jake's hand, dried from the ride over on the stolen bike. "They attacked you?"

"Jumped me at the pub," Jake said. He dusted his knuckles off on the side of his pants.

"Must've thought AJ was there," Richard said.

"AJ will be here," Jake said. "Soon."

Richard hung his head and shook slowly. "They're gonna kill him. Have you seen him?"

"Earlier," Jake admitted. "He'll be here anytime tonight."

Jake went over to the front door and tried to shut it, but it was off one of its hinges and wouldn't stay shut. Even when he forced the lock to tumble, it just barely covered the distance to the doorframe.

"It's got ugly," Richard sighed.

Jake looked back at his dad. He saw the old man he hated, who he dismissed, slumped over with a gun in one hand and his regret-heavy head in the other, unable to turn his face up to the broken kitchen light. He put aside his hate—his rage—for the moment and let a calm sense of pity propel him. The calmness allowed him to mend the door by jiggling it into place.

"Natasha got hold of a statement of ma's accident from the Station. They paid a witness, Gavin Fletcher." He got the door into the right hinge slot and managed to shut it properly. With that closed and the room secured by one barrier, he joined his dad at the table. "That cop, Harvey, paid him to make a false statement. They all work together. The authorities in this town are rotten. They have made it look like AJ committed manslaughter in case any further investigations are to take place." Richard looked up, but the motion of his neck forced a cough out of his throat. "It's a cover-up, and I want that prick Harvey investigated."

Jake noticed that a glass of water was spilled on the floor, likely pushed over in Richard's immediate rise to action. He got up and filled a new one with water from the tap and put it as close to his dad as he could. "Here."

Richard looked down at the water, then up at Jake. "So you have some proof. Have the City authorities arrest this Gavin Fletcher guy. We have a good chance to have them investigate."

"Yeah," Jake said, "well, let's see." Jake turned his head to the door and ground his knuckles into his palm to soothe them.

"I don't think they will be back tonight. Where's AJ?"

"He's collecting the money. He's on a bike." Jake looked at the door again. The attack on the pub was huge, a far bigger force than what came for Richard's humble hovel. It stood to reason they'd need a lot of men on the roads to find AJ if he went out in the brush or dared to cross the flats without lights on. More than they could spare. "Maybe I go look for him."

"Best to wait it out," Richard said. Morning comes, leave. Crash on the couch." Richard straightened himself up in the chair like he would stay there and slurped down some water.

"You look tired," Jake said. "You nod off a bit."

"This would've I've happened," Richard slurred. He put his hands over his face. He felt dreadfully weak, tired, and spent. Jake went to the bathroom in the back to wash his hands clean off his hands and face. He gave himself a good, hard staredown in the mirror, then got distracted by the sight of a pill bottle in the basin. He checked the contents and looked back at his reflection.

Richard did conk out first. Jake put a blanket over him at the kitchen table, where he snored into his forearms. Jake turned out the kitchen light and took a similar neck-aching position. He drifted off to sleep with one eye on the door, waiting for it to open, but it never did...

As the town was partially set on fire and turned upside down, Natasha faced her own adversary, her own title fight. But her fight wasn't a brawl or even a debate. It was a fight for excuses to see how fast she could disengage from her fellow officer's informal advances.

Harvey followed her out with his phone in hand and held it up with the screen bright for her to see. She only barely glanced at it to know that it was nothing she wanted to discuss. Pictures of her at the pub. She already knew what kind of argument he wanted to have and wanted no part in it.

"No," she insisted, "I don't need to look at it."

"Look at it," Harvey insisted right back. "Why lie?"

She stopped in front of her car and turned to him with a snap of her hips. "It's none of your business what I do outside of work, and I have every right to report your strange behavior. How dare you record what I do and with whom I spend my time."

She opened and slammed her car door and drove away. It was her win. Or, perhaps her loss. Harvey was certainly left at a loss for what to do. He could chase her down, but he knew well enough she'd be back. It was her job. She couldn't ignore it forever. She was too honorable.

Harvey paced back toward his car and held his phone up as a light to reach into his pocket for a cigarette. He went to light it up and held the flame out in front of his face for a moment as his eyes adjusted to the light beyond the flame. There was something on the ground, against the front corner of his car, that didn't belong there. Harvey walked around slowly and replaced his lighter with a hand torch that lit up the bloody, caved-in face of Gavin.

"Holy shit."

He stood his ground and inspected the body. Then, the road.

There were no distinct tracks, all the same smudges of tires from cars and bikes that were always in front of the station. Mostly rubber burnt off by his own car making hot pursuits to and from the clubhouse. But he had a policeman's hunch where Gavin's body came from. And who turned him that way.

He took out a cigarette and took a drag of it. The smoke drifted on the wind and dripped down over Gavin's immobile face.

Chapter 32

Jake woke up to a familiar sound that for once wasn't coming from him. The night after any proper fight, and after any victory party out of the hospital, there would be a hideous retching and heaving sound filling his bathroom, or whatever bathroom he had available at the time as his stomach reacted a whole day late to the bludgeoning and hard blows that were given to it. He'd often vomit up anything he ate and drank with a slight coloring of blood in his younger days. As he got older, he vomited less blood but could hold less liquor as a trade-off.

The sounds of violent sick came from the bathroom behind him. He woke up fully and noticed his father wasn't at the table, nor was this blanket. Both, he assumed, were at the toilet. Jake picked himself up and rolled his neck free of kinks to see his father's ill state. Richard was indeed over the toilet; a blanket draped over him like a shawl, a deteriorated old biker acting like a sick old man. He looked over and saw Jake staring down at him with pity.

"Just a reaction from the new pills I'm taking," he said.

"What are they for?" Jake asked.

"Old age," Richard said as he pushed himself up straight.

Jake knew the truth and asked again. "What's with all the medication?"

Richard turned and looked past Jake without a wasted second. "I see AJ didn't make it here last night," he realized. He squeezed past Jake, who did his best not to move, but not to offer any resistance either.

"Why do you need to take them?" Jake asked again. Richard stopped in the short hall into the kitchen. "AJ told me," Jake said affirmatively.

Richard sighed and answered in an annoyed, almost flippant tone. "I have a cancerous tumor as big as a golf ball invading my brain." He shaped it with his finger and tapped it on the side of his head. "I wanted to tell you earlier...It wasn't right; your Mother just died. You were angry and had every right to be angry at me. I'm sorry."

Richard turned away to move on again, avoiding Jake. Jake took his blind spot and hugged the old man from the side. He was so unused to it that, at first, it started as a grapple. He relaxed his arms, took all the rage out of them so that only his sympathy remained. Something close enough to love to make his hug feel real.

"I know. I know you are, Dad." Richard stood still, as did Jake until the moment passed. "Give me an hour. I'll be back. Gather some clothes and prized belongings. Come and keep me and Mom's dog company on the way back to the City."

"What'll I do with my bike?" Richard asked. Jake smirked, not sure if it was a joke or the only real concern Richard had left in his life at that point to care about.

Either way, Jake had a pressing matter to attend to. He raced an eagle across the sky on Gavin's old chopper—not that he'd ever need it again—in the morning sun to the pub. He passed the main entrance and saw two cars out front. One was Mike's, and the other was unknown. The new owners, no doubt. Jake pulled in at the back. He winced as he passed the burnt-out husk of his car shoved haphazardly into the singed garage and parked it in the blood-speckled alleyway.

He got inside and turned on the lights just in time for Mike to start knocking at the door. Jake set up the fallen chairs in the corner and checked over the rest of the floor for any signs of damage. Nothing. Just a few spots where the spittle and blood dried together against the wall, and the dried up blood trail in the back room. He'd left hotel rooms in worse condition before.

Jake opened the door to the always happy Mike and the skeptically pleasant couple that stood behind him. They were expecting someone more professional, less blood-stained, to be answering their call.

"Morning, Jake," Mike said. He extended his hand to lead in the parade of greetings. "Meet the owners." Jake bent forward and shook hands, one by one, and greeted their concerned looks with an understanding smile. "Laura, Jake. Jake, James."

"Come on," Jake offered. He held the inner door open and pushed it all the way, so the springs caught it against the wall. The couple walked in and observed Jake carefully like he was a bouncer. Their eyes wandered around to the rest of the pub. Jake pulled Mike aside before he went off on his own salesman tangent.

"....A little bar fight last night?" Mike asked, pointing to Jake's biggest bruise under his eye. Jake paused, then nodded.

"Mind not going into my Mother's room?" Jake asked. "Packing up her belongings."

"Sure, Jake," Mike said. "I'm sure they will understand. Leave it to me." Jake patted Mike on the shoulder and paced his way to the back room to clean up the worst of the damage. He heard Mike behind him, "Right this way, folks," as he went on with his pitch on how this pub was their best investment, regardless of the state its previous temporary owner was left in.

Chapter 33

It was a busy morning at the Silver City police station. The night's incidents went mysteriously unreported, and all they had to go on were the unsubstantial claims of residents seeing a fire, a bike gang and hearing a single gunshot from various parts of the precinct. Every phone was prone to ringing, and the station's leader was absent in his car on a coffee errand. Natasha sat at Harvey's desk instead, but the presence she felt around her was a severe distraction in her mind. She was behind the desk of, objectively, her enemy. An enemy of the city. Someone she couldn't trust.

The phone rang, and she tensed up. She let it go once out of shock, then picked it up at the start of the second tone. She prepared to make her formal introduction, Silver City Police department, what is the nature of your -.

"You miss me?" Harvey asked. Natasha didn't have time to be shocked that he called his own phone just to check on her. Her mobile phone rang immediately after she answered him. She let it go and held her hand up to the receiver.

"What do you want?" she asked.

There was a pause on the other end, just long enough to

think she had space to speak, but as soon as she opened her mouth, he talked again. "Sounds like someone else misses you?"

She reached into her pocket and put her mobile on silent.

"Mum's calling me again," she said.

"Popular girl," Harvey said slyly. "It's nice to be wanted."

She checked the number. Gold Miner's Pub. Jake.

"Oh, I don't know about that," she said. "Sometimes -."

"You better call your mum back," Harvey said.

"Yes," she agreed, tensely. "I better." She hung up immediately and took out her phone to return the previous call. She was just a minute too late. The phone inside the bar rang while the new tenants were exploring the preparatory room in the back, and Jake wasn't there. He was out front, looking up and down the road, going between a sharp whistle and a loud call.

"Max! Max!? Maaaaaax!"

No sign of the dog in any direction. No signs he'd wandered off either, but the scamp was simply nowhere to be found.

Natasha paced back and forth while she waited for a pickup on the line. She was completely preoccupied with getting in touch with Jake, as he was quick to get in touch with her to let her know just what happened over the night. She finally got through on the next to last ring.

"Hello?" Jake said. He paused. "Natasha?"

Natasha was about to speak when another voice spoke from

the doorway. "Coffee's up," Harvey whispered. Natasha jolted around and nearly knocked the cups out of the cardboard holder he was carrying. He shrank back a bit to protect them and grinned, satisfied at her reaction.

"Oh my God, Harvey!" she exclaimed. The mobile was still against her ear, and she heard Jake over her own panic.

"Natasha? Where are you?" She glanced at the phone and then at Harvey.

"Okay, mum," she said sweetly. "I'll call back later." She disconnected in a hurry and turned to Harvey as he placed the coffees on his desk.

"Don't leave me hanging," he said. She smiled awkwardly and reached for a coffee. He then reached for her, and his hand gingerly overlapped with hers. "The sweet one's mine." Natasha brushed her hand out of his grip and took the other one. "Was rude of you to hang up on your Mother, darling."

"Get over it," Natasha said with a stilted smile. Her mobile buzzed in her hand. Gold Miner's Pub again. She shoved it in her pocket so he couldn't see and made sure to put her attention on him as if it never rang at all. He cocked an eyebrow at her.

"Mummy calling back?" he asked. She just tilted her head and opened her mouth in a half-speaking motion. "Well? Answer it," he obliged.

"It's just mother being needy," Natasha said.

"Don't let me stop you," he offered. "Here, I'll speak to her." He reached for her pocket at first, and she turned away. Then he transitioned to simply holding his hand out patiently.

"Speak to her?" she said anxiously. She laughed the comment off with his smirk. "I'll manage, thank you. Excuse me." She turned and answered the phone and held it close to the side of her head to keep the sounds from leaking out. "Hello, *mother.* Look, I can't talk right now, I'm busy with paperwork -." She turned and rolled her eyes at Harvey, who observed her with cold, calculating eyes.

On the other end, Jake picked up on her scheme and played into it. "Leave now," he said in a whisper. "I'll come by your house and get you -."

Suddenly, a scream. Laura hollered in the back and exclaimed "MY GOD" at the top of her lungs as if she'd just seen a murder scene. As Jake recalled, the ground outside was dirty, but not the frightful mess that would incur that kind of overreaction.

"Leave now," Jake insisted. He hung up and ran to investigate. He ran into the back lot where the hopeful buyers were hunkered over in the corner. Laura was crouched down with her hands over her eyes while the two men tried to nurse her, Mike more timidly and just as distressed as she was.

"Oh my God!" Laura said with a quaking, haunted voice. "Get me outta here now!" James picked her up and led her to the back door. He shot Jake a strange glance, slightly worried and afraid, and Mike went waddling past. Jake looked around to see what could have caused such a scene. The alley was mostly just disheveled, not quite ruined. The bits of blood blended into the gravel below and were unnoticeable.

Then he looked up. He found Max, dangling by his neck from the tree. Jake's arms dropped. His heart dropped. His eyes developed a brief haze as he was bewildered. He could not believe—not even conceive of what he was looking at for a moment. It had to have happened after the brawl while he was with Richard and before he came back.

While Harvey was still on the loose....

Chapter 34

Natasha hung up and went into a desperate rush. She made her way to her desk, snatched her handbag, and made a march for the exit. "I'm going home," she said, desperately."

She was one foot out the door when Harvey came around from behind and grabbed her by the elbow.

"Hey hey hey," he said, trying to be friendly in everything but his grip. "Where do you think you're going? You always lie to your mummy about things?"

"Take your fucking hands off me," Natasha insisted. He tightened his grip on her arm, and she loosened hers on her coffee. It dropped to the floor. Specks of hot water splashed out just as Charlie pulled in and witnessed the scene from out of his window.

"Are you lying to me?" Harvey seethed.

Natasha saw and heard the fury rising beneath his voice, like a growling undertone to his otherwise soft and controlled demeanor.

"You're hurting me, asshole," she said.

"What else have you been lying -."

"Let go of me!" she demanded. She reeled back and stomped on Harvey's foot. He reacted slowly, accepted the pain, and stumbled back a bit. His fury seemed to shield him from the sensation for just a second. Natasha stormed out of the door and bumped past Charlie as he attempted to side-step the coffee puddle. He walked over the cup to Harvey, who adjusted his foot with a gentle roll of his ankle.

"I go get her?" Charlie asked.

Harvey checked his watch and recovered his breathing. "Stay back and mind the station," he said.

Natasha, meanwhile, got in her car and drove non-stop through town to her mum's house in the outer district, far from the center of town. She'd had a hip replacement and could only get around by wheelchair. Her house was well equipped, all one story, but her outings into town required a bit of help.

Natasha intruded as she always did and made her way inside and went straight to the bedroom. She packed all the essentials she could get from hers and her mother's wardrobes and threw it all into a pair of suitcases. Her mother was confused and alert.

"I'll explain details in the car, okay?" Natasha said urgently. "Jake will be here any moment."

She packed everything up in a hurry and paused to catch her breath. Her mum fanned her face with her hand, partially from the rising morning heat and partly from her nerves over the sudden intrusive shift in procedure. It wasn't any normal day-trip they were taking, apparently.

Natasha got everything ready. She put the suitcases out on the front porch and went to her car to get it in place so her mum could get in. It was a whole, long deal to get her mum in and out of the car, just one small hitch that meant time she would be costing Jake—and herself—in the long run.

A bigger hitch was what was in her back seat. A man sprung up before she could scream and put a knife to her throat. One of the bikers from the gang, untouched and unafraid.

"Keep driving," he instructed," and listen to my instructions carefully." Natasha muffled herself to a whimper as she watched the steely blade go close to her neck. She had no choice but to pull away and follow his lead, leaving her mother direly confused.

She'd vanished from the street by the time Jake arrived. He skidded the tires of the motorbike against the pavement and hopped off. He saw two suitcases on the porch and no car in the drive or on the street. Not a sign of her at all, and he knew she wasn't the type to take his panic lightly. He let himself in immediately.

"Natasha!"

His head jerked at the sign of movement. Mum made her way around the corner in her wheelchair. "Jake," she said pleasantly, all the stress drained away once she saw him. "Natasha's just locking up her car in the garage. Come on in."

That was wrong, immediately, because the garage was open outside and there was no car in or near it. He went through the house, calling for her, pushed open the door to the loo and even the crawlspace. Nothing. He ran for the front door and pointed to mum. "Stay in the house," he warned.

"What's going on?" she asked, less worried and more impatient. Jake hopped down the stairs and pulled out his mobile phone. Natasha's buzzed out of her pocket on the passenger's seat. The gangster used his free hand to pick it up. He held it up just to the side of her face so she could see who it was and pressed to answer it.

"Jake!" Natasha exclaimed.

"Focus on driving, bitch," the gangster said. He took control of the phone, much to Jake's rising irritation. "She's one dead bitch if we don't see that money—asshole."

"Where are you?" Jake demanded.

"Drop the cash off at the police station," the gangster instructed. "Have your phone on you."

Jake nearly crushed his phone. His rage refilled. All he could feel was the heat of the sun. He threw himself back onto his bike and ripped across town to the police station. He didn't have the money, but he had a feeling that it wouldn't be going into good hands. The gangster, whether he knew it or not, played a premature hand, and Jake was going to slap the cards right out of it.

Someone would be there to pick up the money, and they'd be in uniform. Whoever it was, they were on the wrong side of the law, and Jake would be the civil enforcer. He stopped in front of the door and let his bike fall on its side. He didn't knock. He punched the door hard enough to rattle the glass pane built into it. His pounding rattled a shovel that was leaned up against the wall. He'd gotten plenty of practice with weapons the night before, so he took that up and used it to break the glass in the window. He scraped the shards out and reached down to unlock the door.

He entered on guard with the shovel in his hands like a baseball bat. "Natasha!" he called. The station seemed empty at first. Then, he heard the final sounds of a commode churning water and the quick steps of someone coming from the hall. Jake held his shovel aloft and saw Charlie walk around the corner. Both of them looked to the desk across the way, with the gunbelt on it. Charlie submitted and held his hands up as Jake approached and lowered his shovel down.

"Where's Natasha!?"

Chapter 35

The clubhouse was abuzz with activity. The members arrived from their pickup routes and brought back a whole person's worth of tradable goods. One of the most expensive commodities for them and groups like theirs, a healthy, organ-filled young woman in ideal condition. They preserved her with a thick black sack over her head so her eyes wouldn't be scarred by the state of their headquarters and kept her hands safe from bruising by tying them up behind her back.

Natasha was left in the dark after she drove up to the clubhouse. The last few yards were dreadful. She was forced to shut her eyes by her hostage-taker and drove blindly up a dirt path toward what she knew was supposed to be an abandoned old truck stop. Not seeing didn't prevent her from not knowing, but she went along for the sake of her own life.

She was the new centerpiece for the main room. The men were all forced to stay away, under strict penalty to keep her from getting spoiled early. She wasn't there for their sake. She was there on the orders of their shadow leader, who arrived shortly after.

Harvey rolled in, in his second uniform, matching the biker garb of Tony's gang, but he commanded far more respect by his face. The members all moved away as he made an unbroken path into the main room. He motioned for one of them to get something from her. Natasha jolted in shock when she felt a hand go into her pocket.

Harvey got a hold of her mobile phone. He intruded into the contact list and searched down to the Js for Jake. He waited for the pickup, thinking that Jake was following his role as the out-of-town patsy he needed.

In the time it took for Harvey to arrive, Jake was already in the police station, a full-on invasive force powered by his unstoppable rage. He squared off with Charlie. The gun belt was closer to the officer, but it wasn't out of range for the faster and more willful Jake. Charlie tried to take a slow, careful step toward the belt on the counter.

"Stay there!" Jake demanded with a jab of his shovel. He moved forward with the handle over his shoulder and the spade aimed at Charlie. He could snap-throw it like a shot put and send it slicing into Charlie's neck. The imagery of such an attack kept Charlie frozen as Jake grabbed the gun and traded it for the shovel. He threw the rest of the belt at Charlie. While Charlie got his pants secure, Jake checked the gun. It was loaded, which Charlie would have known, so he aimed.

"Where's Harvey?" Jake demanded. The sudden shift in his needs caused some confusion in his hostage. Both of them were shaken by the sound of Jake's phone ringing. He held Charlie up with one hand while the other grabbed the phone. Natasha was calling. Jake kept his eyes on Charlie. He looked nebbish and limp, but he was still a cop and one under Harvey's direction. He couldn't be trusted to stay put on fear alone.

"Natasha?" Jake asked.

She didn't answer. "You have the money?" Harvey asked.

Jake huffed aggressively and looked at Charlie. His eyes flickered to other spots in the room, corners and cover, any place he could take advantage of in a sudden scrap.

"Bring her here," Jake demanded, "you get it."

"Put Charlie on the phone," Harvey said. He seemed to know the situation better than Jake expected, though he didn't know it all. He didn't realize who was in control at the station because it certainly wasn't his errand boy. Jake waved Charlie over, then held him up to stop so that he could point the gun at Charlie's forehead. With that fear present, he handed the phone over.

"It's Charlie," the trembling officer said.

"Did he bring the cash?" Harvey asked.

Charlie looked up at the barrel of the gun and Jake's unflinching eyes. "Yes, it's here -."

"Okay," Harvey said pleasantly. "Control the situation. Take out your gun and have him cuffed. Bring him and the money to the clubhouse." He hung up. Charlie handed the phone back over. Jake started to pace around in thought. He tried to keep Charlie in his sights, and the gun pointed in his direction. He plainly didn't have the money and had no way of getting it. Moreover, he didn't trust Harvey or the gang, to be honest. They'd only done wrong by him. No reason to be honorable after all that time.

Jake reached into his pocket with his free hand. It was still there, the beer coaster. He had his dad's phone number but didn't want to take his eyes off Charlie to dial it in. He put it on the corner of a desk and picked up his phone in his off-hand.

"Read the number," Jake commanded. Charlie nodded and listed it off one number at a time. Jake dialed blindly until it was all done, then put the phone to his head and waited. It rang through to the machine. He waited for the beep.

"Hey, I need you right now," Jake said. "I'm at the cop station. They have Natasha." He hung up and slammed his phone face-down onto the desk. He saw Charlie shift in place—maybe to make a run for it, or maybe just to adjust himself to stand more comfortably.

"Stay there!" Jake shouted. "Fuck!" All his rage felt filtered down through his torso and into his arms, but he couldn't swing them to solve his problem. Not yet. So it kept filtering out like steam and reached his fingers where it escaped. His hand that gripped the gun felt the hottest and most bothered.

He had to know why his dad didn't answer, at the most important crossroad of all their lives.

Richard couldn't have answered. He was already listening to something else, his other message on his voice bank, from his other son.

"*Dad, it's AJ. I've buried the cash behind Ma's tombstone. The heat is on me, and I'm waiting this out before I come to see you before I leave...I've seen Jake and mentioned he ought to come see you too. I'm not sure if he's still around but, I don't plan on fucking sticking around.*"

The message sent Richard to his bathroom. Either the nerves of hearing his son's voice in peril or the pills he took made him weak at the knees and even weaker in the stomach. The pills just weren't working by themselves. He took even more and got out of the bathroom to collapse in the hall as he heard the phone ring, then send to messages. He missed his other son's phone call and briefly faded out from the pain.

Chapter 36

The parties were getting ready for a violent convergence. The clubhouse reconfigured itself to receive the new visitor. The members moved Natasha into another room with shielded windows and a layer of dust that kicked up with every pushing, shuffling step.

Tony got to oversee the operation. He was disgruntled and a bit put-off. His men were all being ordered around on Harvey's word instead of his own, and it was starting to get to him. It was all toward the same end, getting back the money and goods, but it didn't feel like he was doing enough. He handled Natasha a bit rougher than the other members did and let her fall on her side to the floor. He bent down to take off her head cover when one of the men burst through the door.

"Need you in here for a second," the member said. Tony stood up and pointed for him to take over.

"Keep an eye on her," he said. The member nodded and took over in the room. Tony wandered over where a small group gathered around at a safe distance. From one hostage problem to another.

AJ was on the floor, clutching his stomach, with a bloody

knife just an arm-length away. Tony sighed and looked around. The other members looked upset and defensive.

"He pulled a knife on us," one of them said. Tony believed them and stepped forward. He planted his boot firmly on the dagger, and the rest of his men swooped in to pull AJ onto his feet. They brought him over to a safer spot and checked him over while Tony went out to inspect the front of the yard. They were expecting company soon.

That company was stalled at the bottom of the hill, just off the outlet road from the highway, out of sight. Jake sat in the passenger seat with Charlie at the wheel under the threat of instant death should he stray from the path. They were just within range of the clubhouse.

Jake unloaded the gun and checked the chamber. It hadn't even been primed, so he was good to leave it as it was. He reached into the backseat and grabbed a fabric bag he had brought along. He ejected all the rounds into it, then slid the empty magazine back in and snapped the slide forward. It was empty, not useless, but far less dangerous in Charlie's hands.

The only play Jake had was to play his part in the grand scheme and let Charlie play the role of captor. They rode up to the outskirts of the clubhouse until the truck stop was just in sight at the edge of the parking yard. Jake handed over the gun and held his grip on the barrel until Charlie looked him in the eyes. He expressed his intent without words and shook the deputy in his seat.

They got out and assumed the position. "Confidence, yeah," Jake whispered as he put his hands on his head. Charlie held him up with the fake gun in an assertive, stiff pose. "Do as I told you." Charlie prodded him in the back and forced him forward. They entered through the gates and strode up to the front of the building. From within, Jake could hear a gangster cat-calling his arrival. "The motherfucker," they shouted. "Well, well, look what the cat dragged in!"

Jake leaned his head to the side. The wind was soft and warm. The distance whispered with the sounds of restless bush and the faint hum of an engine on the road, close enough to be heard but still too far away from the dark world. Jake entered to help.

In the back, Tony and the other members brought AJ to the room next to Natasha to keep him separate from the rest of their space. Harvey burst through in full garb with a retinue of a few Southeast Asian members following his motions rather than his direct words. He squatted down and grabbed AJ by the chin, which caused him to uncurl from his dire position, and made the bloodstain on the front of his shirt more visible.

"A little accident?" Harvey said. "Did you not learn from your first mishap that your actions have consequences?" He looked over to the other hostage on the floor, who raised her covered head to try and stay alert to what was going on. Harvey turned his attention back to AJ. "Are we ready?" he shouted. He took his hand away and let AJ's head fall back to the floor. Then he poked his finger on AJ's temple. "Not too much thinking going on up here, huh?"

He hopped up to his feet and swung his arm to the door. "Everyone out," he commanded. The members exited, even the ones who didn't understand him. Tony stepped out last and glanced at Harvey, not in question but a more subtle demand that he better do things right. Harvey waited for him to be gone before he crouched down deep, almost in a crawl, next to Natasha's head.

He whispered to her, in a sinister tone, "Let's see how your little mixed martial artist LOVER," he suddenly shouted, causing her to jerk in place, "makes his way out of this one." He stood back up and turned to leave. As if at his own summoning, Charlie entered with Jake in his possession.

The members swarmed the front door to inspect the situation. One of them chimed off, "Good job, Charlie," and circled to Jake's front. He had a dent in his forehead that looked unnatural. Jake glared down at him and recognized him easier in the light. He looked like one of the guys he'd beaten the hell out of the night before, and the gangster seemed overjoyed to see him again.

"Hell, I've been saving up a lot for you," he said as he rolled his knuckles into his palm. The other members from that night spread out, all with eyes full of vengeance for him. "Before you take him in there, do me the pleasure and keep that GUN pointed at his fucking head." The rest of the crew smiled, all at the prospect that the gun might be loaded. "Nothing you can do about this now, eh fucker? I'll even give you a chance and count it in for ya. Ready? One -."

He held Jake's shoulder and wound his other hand back in a fist.

"Two."

He clenched his fist hard. Jake was utterly ambivalent. It was such an amateurish punch. Even if it took it to the face, it wouldn't knock him out, but it would rattle his teeth or crack his nose. He was blending in just fine with his nose unblocked.

"And Three!"

And he'd be damned if he let a bunch of salty bastards put him on the mat. He side-stepped the punch at the last second. As he turned, the gangster lunged forward and was further yanked by his hand on Jake's moving shoulder. Charlie took the blow instead, right to the face, and it knocked him out of the door back onto the pavement. The member fell forward on top of him as well.

Jake lowered his arms. No more blending in. He rolled his shoulders and turned to see the rest of the welcoming party scrambling for whatever weapons were nearby.

Two exhibition matches in a row. No title fights, no high stake cards. His career really was over....

Chapter 37

Harvey set himself up in the holding room with Natasha in the corner. Before he dealt with her, he dealt with himself. He was coasting off of a few highs already, but not the most important one. He lined up a solid, thick line of powder on a clean table and dragged it in. It made him feel stronger, more confident, more cocksure. He made a few quick sniffles as he headed over to Natasha and started to ungag her. He yanked off the black bag and pulled off the gaffer tape around her mouth. She shouted in pain. He lowered himself down to her level. She spat on his face. He didn't even flinch.

"Not nice," he said.

"You fucking monster -."

Harvey shushed her with a gentle press of his middle finger to her lips. "I really cared about you," he said. "And I've never cared for anyone."

Natasha struggled and pulled herself away from his sweaty leather glove. "Get away from me, you fucking creep!"

Harvey chuckled. "What? Creep!?" He smiled wide. White crumbs speckled the front of his mustache. His eyes were already going bloodshot. Natasha turned away from him. He grabbed her by the cheek and forced her eyes forward. "Look at me! I fucking knew you were fucking him -."

She spat again, and Harvey didn't just let it go. He reeled his hand back and slapped her. She took it with a stern grunt.

"Why you -."

"We know," she began, "you had his mother killed! We know you paid for a false statement! And now the City authorities know. And now you know you're all fucked."

Harvey stood up and drew out a gun with a quick, jerky movement. He knelt back down and held it against her head. Natasha was frozen in fear. All she heard was Harvey's shaky, angry breathing and the sounds of something else in the distance. The thumps and thuds of what sounded like a brawl were happening out in the front of the club.

Further away, near the garage, Tony was sitting with his ear pressed hard to a phone. He tried to get away to some peace and quiet, to think and to manage his gang, but the gang was getting in the way. Some of the boys were having too much fun and were laughing over what seemed to be an important phone call. He turned to them with a stiff hand stretched out.

"Quiet!" he demanded. The boys looked his way and saw him on the phone. "Quiet," he said, more politely. The members all nodded and got up to leave. Tony turned back to the phone and listened closer. "Speak up, Richard. You sound hoarse."

"Come collect the money," Richard said on the other end, "at front gates of the cemetery. Bring my sons." Tony smirked as the call disconnected. He stood up and grinned with a wistful, nostalgic look in his eyes.

Meanwhile, to get his nerves even more flared and furious, Harvey snorted another line with a pistol in his hand. Natasha looked end to end across the room for some chance to escape, just one opening she could take to crawl out. AJ was down and out and looked seriously hurt. Whatever was happening in the other room didn't seem like it was getting closer.

"Tell me," Harvey demanded, dementedly, "what has that fucker got that I haven't? Really, you think -" Just as Harvey was about to try and make a point, someone knocked at the door. The knocking was loud and forceful, not the kind of normal members made. He went to answer it and looked up to see Tony standing with a smug smile on his face.

"Is he here?" Harvey asked, teeth gritting in frustration.

"No!" Tony exclaimed. "It's his old man, Richard. He's got the cash. He wants an exchange for his sons." They both turned their eyes toward AJ, who laid, faded out and pale on the floor. They moved in to collect him but were interrupted once again as one of the members skidded to a stop in front of the open door.

"He's here!" the gangster exclaimed. The men looked at one another. Then they finally heard it, three rooms away. The crash of something—or someone—being run through a wall.

Jake was in the midst of a brutal fight. It started simple enough. Though he lacked the backup from the night before, it was the same song and dance, a Kumite, one against many alleyway brawls. This time he had more of an environment. The floor was slick and dusty and covered with old plastic tile panels. Underneath that was a solid wooden frame floor, and underneath that were pipes and wires. The walls were drywall and lumber. The shelves were all thin metal and were mostly broken to reveal sharp jagged edges.

He wasn't in the eight-sided ring anymore. He had to watch every angle at all times, react to the highest levels of danger first, and sacrifice his body to the least dangerous blows as a means of passive defense. First, he dealt with the threat from behind. The gangster that fell on Charlie took the gun and aimed it triumphantly at Jake's face. Jake turned and saw the empty barrel staring him in the eye.

"You're a dead man, fucker!" the thug shouted.

Jake nodded. "Yes, you are."

The gang all started laughing until they heard the empty click. It shocked the one holding it the most. Jake used his shock as an opportunity. He threw a palm strike to the man's hand and smacked it against the wall. The back of his hand was sandwiched between the hard metal and the hard wall immediately, causing him enough pain to drop it. Then he jabbed his knee into the thug's crotch to stagger him. Once he was off-balance, Jake performed a turn-around side-roundhouse—a risky move against an alert and active opponent, but a perfect full-body gut check to the unprepared—and sent the thug back-first into a dent in the wall.

That set the tone for the first few movements of the fight. At first, the only men smart enough to avoid Jake were two Asian men who retreated to the back wall while the others charged with wooden planks and baseball bats. They swung wide and hard. Their recovery was awful. Jake pressed his attack as soon as one of them missed with short, sharp liver jabs that went under their ribs and made them feel sick. It gave him a few seconds while they were stunned to strike the others.

He moved blearily fast, like a bike overtaking at 120kph from an idle vehicle on the side of the road. The gangsters were no match without coordination. Two of them tried to flank Jake and press their own advantages. One wielded a knife and stood behind Jake. The other had a chain and swung it loosely to wrap him up. Jake rolled. It was a flashy, useless skill most of the time, a mid-recovery from a grounding blow, but it was so unexpected that it worked, and he ended up behind the chain wielder who didn't have time to swing. He reached forward, grabbed the leg, jerked his body, and swung the man to the ground like a sandbag.

The knife-wielder remained confident, despite his lack of reach. Jake remained on the floor, back flat, palms down, one leg up. The thug advanced with a blade in hand. Jake snap-kicked him in the gut and planted his foot back down as the guy stumbled back into the wall. Just because he was on the ground didn't mean he couldn't fight. He was safer there, with his legs giving him reach, than if he were standing.

Jake rolled forward to his feet, lunged with one deep step, and performed a standing jump into a dropkick. His feet planted against the man, and the man planted against the shelf. The shelf, and the opponent, gave way. Jake managed to land in a deep squat and stood back up. There were still two left, the Asian men who stood back and observed the whole time.

One struck a Muay Thai pose, fists vertically up, elbows out, and leg forward. The other took a more traditional karate stance but had his stance low and shoulders loose, something more akin to a soft grappling style. He'd dealt with traditional martial arts before. Under the rules, they could strike, swing, grab and grapple. All of their tools were on the ready, unlike in a boxing or wrestling ring. With no rules, however, they lacked a crucial defense.

Jake stood up, slumped forward, arms loose and legs bent with his center of gravity pushed forward a bit. He looked lazy and slumping like he was either drunk or about to fall over. Most importantly, his face was exposed—or so he wanted them to think. They both advanced together, shouting war cries as they did. The first kicked at Jake's face. Jake simply straightened his posture, and it was like he retreated three whole feet. Before the kick ended, he swung his arms up and grabbed the man by the ankle.

Jake tugged back with all his force and swung the man fully over his shoulder. He felt the leg disconnect somewhere as he swung it like he was throwing a bag of garbage into a can overhead—or like he was swinging a pickaxe with the intent of breaking it off at the handle. The man's face met the ground, and he was incapacitated. The other guy took advantage and hit Jake from behind.

It was a solid rib blow. Jake delivered a spinning backhand, which was deftly avoided. He resumed a boxing stance as the karate fighter returned to his pose as well. A few blows ensued as they tested one another's range and power. Jake had the upper hand in both, but his opponent lacked openings. The blows were shallow because he was baiting for a grab. Jake slid his foot forward to try and catch his enemy by the ankle, but the karate expert stepped to the side and easily faded away.

"Could go pro," Jake said. The man didn't reply or possibly even understand. He threw a quick punch, which Jake caught in one hand. The fist slipped out. Too sweaty, and Jake was getting weak. His breath couldn't keep up with him anymore. His rage wasn't enough to fill his lungs or his brain with oxygen. He was fading. He needed one good blow to change the tide.

He punched. The Asian fighter caught him and began the twisting maneuvers to get him into a throw. That's just what Jake wanted. He felt his body get pulled with his momentum, so he jumped up and swung his leg hard as he went forward. He got thrown away just as he connected, and both fighters went tumbling to the floor. Jake recovered first and scrambled forward. He stomped hard but only hit the floor as his opponent rolled away. Jake spun around to catch his on the rise and saw, out of the corner of his eye, that the fight was already over.

Someone was intruding on the ring. It was no longer a simple fight. It turned into a negotiation.

Chapter 38

Tony and Harvey stood in the hall connecting to the storefront of their clubhouse. Tony held AJ by the back of his bruised neck and made him move on his legs with squeezes and pinches from behind. Harvey led Natasha out with a gun at her back. Jake assumed that it was a loaded gun, that Harvey wouldn't be clever or merciful enough to pull a similar gambit. Natasha didn't even know where she was with the cloth back over her face, but she could tell what was happening.

Jake held his position and started breathing fast. Tony entered the fray and started kicking the men Jake put on the ground to stir them up. Most just moaned and added the stiff strike into the long list of their pains. The two Asian men got up. The Muay Thai fighter was noticeably unstable.

"Time to go," Tony said. He patted the fighters on their backs and led them back into the hall.

Harvey stepped forward and made himself the center of attention. "Nice bluff," he said to Jake, "and I seriously hope to God your old man doesn't disappoint." He turned to Tony and jittered his head to the side. "He stays here." Tony looked at Jake and shrugged. "Take the old man for a long ride," Harvey instructed, "and do away with him."

Tony kicked AJ in the back of his knees and let him fall face-first to the ground. The Asian fighters took Tony's side and left out the front door. Another member crawled up to his feet to join them. "You!" Harvey shouted. "Where'd you think you're going? Not finished. Come here." The member looked at Harvey and the gun he wielded and joined him. He saw the laser-focused hate the co-leader had for Jake, and the simmering, burning rage that Jake still had over nearly everyone in sight.

Just up the road, Tony arrived in an uncovered junker of a Jeep with his two men and had them keep the engine running while he approached his old friend again. Richard had both black bags, which were dusted with dirt. He looked ages older than he did, even just a few days ago. No sleep, no food, and no time left. Tony's smirk faded when he saw him, past his prime and one foot in the grave.

He patted Richard down as a formality. Found nothing. "Drop the bags, arms out," he insisted. Richard followed, checked the sleeves of Richard's jacket, and found them worryingly thin. He thought he felt bone wrapped in leather instead of flesh. Everything was clear. Tony grabbed the bags and put them on the bonnet of the car to check them out.

"Where's my boys?" Richard asked.

Tony unzipped the bags to check them over. He found the money, and he found the drugs. Everything was back on track. "I told you," he said, "you were the brains of the family." He handed both over to his retinue sitting in the passenger's seat, who passed it to the other man in the back. Tony patted the car door, signaling the man in the back to climb up to the front.

"Righto…."

"Where's my sons?" Richard demanded.

The car left. It was just Tony and Richard at the moment. "On the back," Tony said. He walked over and mounted up the Harley Richard came on.

"We had a deal," Richard insisted.

"Yeah, yeah," Tony said flippantly.

"Take me to them," Richard pleaded. "Are they alive?"

Tony looked up, disappointed, and sighed. "Yes. Now. Let's go somewhere nice and quiet and chat about a few things before you go see 'em." Tony looked over the bike. He couldn't find a way to start it. Richard approached, weakly, with his helmet in his hands.

"You need the key to start," he said.

Tony held his hand out. "Give it to me," he said. He waited to feel the touch of keys in his palm. He turned just as Richard took his pistol out from the lining in his helmet. A cold silence passed.

Then, a gunshot. It was heard back at the clubhouse. Harvey was patrolling the storefront between Jake and Natasha, who the gang member held up.

"That can't be good," Harvey said. He looked over at Jake, whose eyes were full of heat and light. Full of rage.

"You had my mother killed," Jake huffed.

Harvey shook his head with a taciturn smile. "Don't you

point your finger at me. It was an accident." Harvey turned his finger to AJ on the ground. "He did it to her. He did it to your family. He's to blame." He returned to Natasha's side and pulled off her cover again. She and Jake met eyes. He saw her concern, and she saw his stalwart determination. It calmed her if only a little bit.

Her worry returned as Harvey stood between them, wide-eyed, and hopped up on powdered delusions. "You both read the statement, yes?" he shouted. "Did you read the fucking report!? YES!?"

"I know the truth -."

"You did read it, yes?" Harvey insisted, punctuating every syllable with force.

"You paid Gavin Fletcher," Jake accused, "to falsely claim to have witnessed the accident. That I know -."

"That you know!?" Harvey exclaimed. "You don't know shit. Yes!" He started rocking his head around like he was being shaken. "Gavin Fletcher!" He did a quick cross of Christ motion from his shoulders to his head, but it eventually spiraled out into a limp-wristed circle. "May he rest in peace. His body….DUMPED brutally at my car. Evidence points to you." He ended his motions with a slow point at Jake. AJ looked between his brother and Natasha from his place on the floor.

"Highly likely you murdered him," Harvey said. "In fact— you did! You did me a favor!" Harvey chuckled and pulled out a vial from his pocket, full of powder. He opened it up to his nose, closed his other nostril, and sniffed until all that was left inside was what clung to the bottom in a cakey layer. He breathed deep as he let the load hit the back of his head.

"I couldn't've planned it better myself. I could easily have you both put behind bars." He motioned back to Natasha with a toothy grin. "I'm looking forward to chatting to the city authorities." Then he returned to Jake. "We have the witness, Mr. Gavin fucking Fletcher. However, the witness was murdered by the Son of the deceased Mother. Case closed." He whipped around quickly and pointed to the member. "Keep that gun on her!"

"To protect-" Jake started.

"Enough!" Harvey screamed. He waved his arms wildly in the air as if the whole room was screaming at him. "SHUT UP!" He held his ground for a moment and paused. Waited for the nothing to calm down. Then he looked up at Jake. "I don't believe in an even playing field. And this is my field." Harvey took a fighting stance, a hopping boxing pose, as traditional as it came. "Keep that gun on her," he mumbled. Jake gave Natasha a passing glance as if she was a member of the audience. He could let her know he was fighting for her, but at this point, it'd be a lie.

That wasn't how he went into the ring.

"I believe," Harvey said, "We both feel a common hate for each other—yes?"

Jake put his arms up. He agreed with Harvey but with a caveat. What Jake felt wasn't justifiable as just hate. It was rage.

Chapter 39

At the edge of the graveyard, past the swinging gates, was a dead body. It didn't quite get into the yard to be buried where it belonged. A set of tire tracks tore away from the dirt path to the road. A small pool of blood seeped into the dry dust of the outback under Tony's face. Richard ran the route back to the clubhouse, hoping to get there before the deal was sealed. The gang wouldn't need the boys if they had the bags.

As one duel was sealed and closed, another was about to start. Harvey overdosed on all kinds of blow, but he held his ground with a professional stance. He switched between classic upright boxing and a low, southpaw stance. His footwork was as rapid as his heartbeat. He had energy to spare. In any other circumstances, Jake would have him pegged as a rope-a-dope and run out the clock. But he knew better.

There was no bell and no timer, no commercial breaks. Just two men, their bodies, and their breaking points. Jake was already a few rounds down with injuries. Harvey was fresh and drugged up. There were always suspicious matches, guys who limped to the dressing room and came out nearly dancing, but they were subtle and unspoken. It was a quiet secret in the world of pros. Some people did it, and at length, they got caught.

Jake squared up his shoulders, firmed his grip on the ground, and held his fists up. He was bigger and stronger than Harvey but hurt. He had everything to lose. His captive audience secretly rooted for him. He even felt the approval of the man with the gun, who was more afraid of Harvey than he was hateful of Jake.

Harvey started the fight. He landed between his hops and stepped in. He was moving faster than normal. Whatever stopped him from going that fast normally was turned off deep in his brain. He threw a few punches into Jake's guard and got closer enough to slip past it. Jake took a hook that went all the way around his arms. He blocked the next one, but Harvey used the small moment where he made the gap in his protection to throw a straight to Jake's face. It was fast and firm but hollow. Snappy, stinging. Not solid blows with follow-through, just taps, and slaps. Heat and pain.

He was strong, but Jake had more than strength on his side. He had experience. Technique. Harvey was just a flurry of blows. Jake knew how to deal with that type of fighter. It was as easy as a faint, a fade, and a quick series of blindsides. He leaned to the right just as Harvey punched with his left hand, leaving him exposed and unprepared. Harvey followed the act and raised his guard as Jake's left hook came dangerously close to his face. It was a fake-out. Jake used his swinging hand to jerk his body up into a flying knee on the left side of Harvey's groin, right in the pivotal place in the pelvis.

A normal opponent would have bent over to rebalance themselves or get sick from the low blow. It was an improper blow in full-contact sport fighting. Anything on or around the trunks was considered a foul. Jake felt liberated fighting without rules. There were so many techniques he could pull out that were normally sealed away with no refs or bells or fences. Jake stomped his foot down, planted his legs, and threw a punch.

Harvey faded back. He leaned and nearly fell over but caught himself and hopped back in a mad-looking twisting leap. Then he came forward with another series of straights at Jake's face. Jake ducked and landed a solid lean-in blow to Harvey's gut, expecting him to fold up and seize, but no chance. Harvey started hammering Jake right on his spine through his muscles.

Jake fell and rolled. Harvey stomped the ground. He jumped and stomped both feet onto a fractured piece of plastic that broke under his heels. Jake pushed himself up and recovered. He saw Harvey hopping forward with his leg wound back for a kick. Jake rolled away and just avoided it, then stood back up, arms tucked in, pre-emptively blocking. Harvey came in with a haymaker that missed. Jake reached up and grabbed Harvey by his short hair, but his fingers lost grip.

The rage was all he had. Not energy, not motivation. Harvey still had energy to spare, artificial though it was, and had no bottom in sight. As soon as he was free, he swung around with a sweeping sidekick that Jake easily dodged. Harvey's movements were blunt and sloppy, but he could make as many as he wanted without the risk of slowing down. Jake could already feel parts of his body going numb. He had his arms under control, but his hands were getting softer. He couldn't rely on traditional grabs. But he still had his arms.

Harvey swung wide again. Jake followed through with a mid-body grapple. Harvey struggled out of it easily, but it pushed him to the ground, right where Jake wanted him. Jake dove onto Harvey's back and wrenched his arm underneath Harvey's head to get at his neck. A reverse pinning chokehold. Harvey immediately thrashed himself back on top, but Jake remained pinned in place, one stiff arm pressing Harvey's throat from the front while Jake locked his neck straight from behind.

All that Jake needed was time. No matter how much blow or adrenaline was in Harvey's system, it was still flowing through a human body. With the blood supply cut off from his brain, and the air from his lungs, he'd be out in a matter of minutes. Eternity in the ring, but in such a messy brawl, it was plenty of time to wait. Harvey wasn't so far gone that he forgot his place and not too delusional to believe that getting choked from behind was a place he could easily escape. He was desperate to get out. He opened his hands and reached back to try and pry the sweaty arm off. Then he reached behind his head and tried to scratch Jake's face up.

It was uncouth, to say the least, in a fight to resort to that level of desperation. It informed Jake of just how far gone his opponent truly was and how right he was to keep the pressure on. What he didn't account for, however, was his lower half. His face was well defended against an attack, but he neglected to lock Harvey's legs in place. Once he realized, he scrambled to wrap his legs around Harvey's thigh in a lock. Harvey realized it at the same time and bucked both his legs high up.

Jake was just a little taller than Harvey and longer in the

torso. His groin rested slightly below Harvey's. Jake tucked his knees up to prevent his testicles from getting a double-heel-drop. Harvey's boots landed on Jake's knees, not even halfway through the crushing momentum they needed. Their position expanded. The space between their back and front turned into an arcing bridge, like an eye slowly opening. Harvey's chin shortened, and Jake couldn't keep his grip anymore as the weasley bandit finally slipped out of the grip.

Jake tried to lock him into another submission, but Harvey scrambled away. "Give me the gun!" Harvey shouted to his confidante. The member looked confused. Jake scrambled after Harvey. They were engaged in a ground game, whether he liked it or not. He grabbed Harvey's feet, both of them, and whipped him like he was unfolding a sheet. Then he ascended his grip and grabbed Harvey's thighs, ready to put him in a front-facing rolling lock from behind. Harvey thrashed and managed to twist one leg out. His heel just barely caught Jake's chin.

Jake dove once more just as Harvey got up. They were standing but in the same position, rear chokehold, tighter than before. Jake wasn't going for a tap out or count down. He went for the immediate kill. Collapse the throat, and if possible, snap the neck.

"Shoot him!" Harvey gurgled.

The gun-wielding member had his hand forward but was shaking. He'd watched the bloodiest spectacle of violence he'd ever seen from a safe distance. The sight of Jake's fighting filled him with an exciting rush, as it did with all his audience.

And the fact that he did it to the boy's boss added a quake of fear into his muscles.

"I can't get a clear shot!" he exclaimed.

Amid the standoff, the member caught sight of Jake's eyes. He wasn't focusing on his chokehold or Harvey. His rage was directed at the biker in front of him. As if he was broadcasting through his glare that once Harvey fell, he'd be next, and he'd somehow get it worse.

All three of them, in their battle-lust, forgot about the hostages. And through all of their dealings, in confidence, they neglected to disarm Natasha of her heels. She stomped the member in the boot. Her stiletto point crumpled the top of the thick leather shoe and made him drop the gun on the ground. He fell back, and she followed up with a hopping kick to his groin.

Harvey's eyes focused entirely on the gun. Jake's arms focused entirely on knocking him out. The two of them were bound, and Jake didn't need the gun to finish the job. Harvey did. The only one in sight to get it was Natasha. She lunged forward and tripped. She crawled for the gun to get it and turn the tide.

A boot beat her to it. A fourth party, forgotten even by Jake after the long fight. The one guy in the parlor he didn't personally knock out. It was Charlie. He woke up, face bloody from the punch he took and picked up the gun with Natasha at his feet. He pointed the gun at Natasha and turned to Jake. Jake met eyes with him. There was a rage in Charlie that he couldn't ignore.

Jake let go, and Harvey dropped flat to the ground, blacked out. It didn't last long. Most tap-out submissions are only a few seconds long at most; Jake knew that. The best chokehold would either make a man go limp or make him die. Jake was still minutes off from death. He had a technical victory, but in the lawless land he was in, it didn't mean shit.

Chapter 40

Harvey awoke with a sputter and a cough. Charlie held the room up with the only loaded gun. It didn't matter if he was a worse fighter, he was in control, and he knew it. The member who formerly owned the gun, as gutless as he was, writhed on the ground with his hands over his injured groin. He was, for the most part, out of action. Charlie turned his gun to Natasha.

"Up!" he commanded. "Now!" She stood up slowly, so he grabbed her arm and forced her along. Harvey returned to consciousness fully, still pumped up on blow and a heavy dose of testosterone from the fight, and stretched his neck. He saw the situation and nodded his head.

"Nice one, Charlie," he commented. He went over, and Charlie immediately surrendered the gun to him. "Go get your car." Charlie agreed and ran out the front, hopping over bodies in his way. Jake watched him go and immediately felt his head spin and sink. He was overcome with exhaustion. All his rage had been spent, and what was left was deflated along with his will to fight with the presence of a gun in play.

He thought he was spent—until he saw Harvey put the gun up to Natasha's head. He still had enough rage and stood up.

"Just let her go," he demanded. Harvey grinned wide.

Charlie made his way outside and went to his car. He was finally in control of it again, not held up against his will. He noticed a black bag was outside the driver's side door and checked the contents. It was loaded with cash. He knelt and pondered for a moment what to do. All the criminals were inside the clubhouse, either dressed as gangsters or unfortunate civilians. He was the only cop on sight, and the city officials were on their way thanks to Natasha's tip-off.

He could just take the money and leave them all high and dry. They'd come back into town on bikes and get arrested, and he could lock them up while the city cops did the booking. He had a perfect out. Then, as if to punish him sheerly for the thought, he heard a gunshot come from inside. Someone was dead. Was it Jake? Natasha? He wasn't sure who else Harvey could shoot.

Charlie forgot about AJ, the man on the wanted poster, who had run from the terrible fight holding his blood in and met Charlie from behind with a tight chain around the neck. AJ was inspired by Jake's fighting spirit and filled with a rage of his own. He wrapped the chain around Charlie's neck, then hoisted him up over his back, so the cop's legs dangled off the ground. Charlie reached and scratched for freedom around his neck, but it was too tight and too hot. He lost his breath first, then his consciousness and AJ kept him held up until he stopped moving completely.

AJ looked back at the clubhouse, then down to the uniformed officer.

Inside, Harvey stood with his arm stretched out over Natasha's back. Natasha was left mortified as she watched the steady trickle of blood pour out of the guts of the member's body. She'd only hurt him, but Harvey had no qualms killing just to show off he could. He turned to Jake and pointed the gun back down at Natasha.

"Let that be an example," he growled, "I'm serious! You try being a hero again, and I'll end your life sooner than you would like."

Jake took a series of deep, frustrated breaths and ultimately soothed himself to a steady calm. There was nothing he could do but be grateful that Harvey's want for theatric panache seemingly clouded his very real desire for slaughter. As long as Harvey stayed manic and overly confident, Jake and Natasha were safe as hostages. It was when he calmed down that Harvey would be truly dangerous.

Jake turned to the shop entrance and saw the car slowly amble up. Harvey waved his gun for Jake to go out. Natasha followed out with her hair clamped in Harvey's grasp. "Front page would say this... event would go down as a massacre? Gang-related? Many would be convinced that was the case." Harvey circled to the left side with Natasha while Jake lingered on the right and glanced down at the driver in his hat and blue shirt. "Another turf war," Harvey continued. "Rival gang members trying to reach the pinnacle of who's better in a hierarchy of gang war stupidity. Just facilitating, stabilizing, this chaotic landscape...the devil is in the details. Neither of you would have to go through the stress of it all." He waved Jake over to the passenger door. "Soon, you'll be dead."

Jake got in and had the door slammed nearly against him. He glanced at Charlie—at AJ, who'd taken Charlie's clothes and kept his eyes covered and dead ahead. Jake stifled himself before he made so much as an acute breath. He went with the flow and stayed as calm as he could. Harvey opened the back door and was greeted by a seat filled with a black duffle bag.

"Well, well," he said. He unzipped the top and checked the contents. He was pleased. He zipped it back up and grabbed it, then replaced it with Natasha. "In you hop," he gingerly commanded. Once she was in, not even seated, he slammed the door. Jake looked over to AJ, who kept himself dead ahead and focused. His breathing was slow and reasonable. His skin was a bit pale from the blood loss, but he covered it with the deep-tucked brim of the hat. Natasha noticed him next, in the rearview mirror from the backseat.

Harvey tapped on the roof of the car. "Open the boot, Charlie," he instructed. AJ moved his face away and his hand down to the boot opening button. Harvey walked back to see the boot as it opened, then stopped, just a bit short. He circled back to the front of the car and poked against the window at Jake. "Get out," he said. "In the boot. Now."

Jake gave AJ a single glance of trusting approval. He got out and met Harvey at the rear of the car. He walked slowly. He was on the defense. The battle wasn't over, not with his brother in his corner. Harvey remained completely positive. He still had the gun, but he knew nothing. Even in the boot, if they took off, Jake would be far safer, and Harvey would be abandoned, surrounded by a mountain of evidence of his crimes.

Harvey patted the boot lid. "Now, I said," he insisted. Jake stood still, unmoving. Harvey turned to the car. "I said open the boot!"

AJ pressed the button. The boot unlocked and slowly rose through the hydraulic hinges. Harvey looked down with sinister glee, which was cut short by a moment of confusion. He looked down and saw two bags. One more than he expected, both unzipped. He looked at the bag in his hand, thinking he lost it, or it wasn't even there in the first place, but it was.

He looked back to see a hand stick out of the other bag. A frail hand that held a handgun. As he was held up, it occurred to him that he hadn't seen or heard from Tony since the bags came back. Who else could have dropped them off? "Oh, Fuck...."

Harvey was shot through the throat. His hands immediately dropped what he was holding, and he reached up to try and contain the massive wound. He was already dying, as good as dead, but that wasn't good enough for Jake. He sprung, tackled Harvey to the ground, and beat his arms until they were limp and his face until it was frozen. Then he snaked his way to get his legs around the neck. Jake had a history with the move, the Python Grip Scissor Neck Submission Hold. It was so dangerous that it was immediately banned from all professional matches the first time he used it. Unlike an arm-based headlock, the legs were stronger and harder to break free. It was a sure win, but it was also deadly. And he was doing it to a man with a hole through his throat.

AJ and Natasha jumped out of the car and went to the back

to see what had occurred. They ignored the bloody spectacle on the ground and turned to the man who came crawling out of the bag in the boot. It was Richard. He'd returned unannounced and positioned himself as a last gambit, either knowing or smartly guessing that Tony's partner would try to place the bags in the boot before driving off. They helped Richard out just in time to watch his son fight on the ground.

The other thing about the Python Grip hold was its sheer unfairness. There was nothing Harvey could do. Jake was above him, straddling his shoulders and crushing his neck with his thighs. Jake's lower legs were stretched out enough to lock down Harvey's shoulders so he couldn't reach up above his head at all. All Harvey had left was his lower body, but every movement he made to flop or flounder around was wasted because his neck was completely immobilized. He could twist as much as he wanted from his waist. Jake was too stable to move or twist away. Jake just sat in both a pool of pouring blood and his rage as he watched the maniac cop die.

Then, things went quiet. There was no bell for the victor, no announcer naming a champion. The heat in Jake's body came mostly from the blood that covered his lower half. The pain he felt came from a lifetime of fighting. All brought to a hideous climax. The light was the sun and the glint of the car. He pushed himself away and laid down on the ground, more tired than he'd ever been in his life, as his family surrounded him. He saw Natasha, the family he'd always wanted. AJ, the family he wished he never forgot. And Richard, the family he never knew he needed so badly.

Chapter 41

Jake entered a bright, stagnant room. The lights were bright and clean. He still felt the pain from his sprains and bruises. He was good to walk and come and go as he pleased, but despite that, he remained close by at the hospital for the people who couldn't get up and go as easily. He walked down the hall, head down and hands stowed away, and checked in on his dad once more.

The entire ordeal was long over. Things were settled and evened out. Mountains of evidence, testimony, and rewarding political favors kept Jake out of a cell and out of the papers. He was written up for the bar fights, all acting in defense of his family's left-behind legacy, and his brother's charges were suspended due to the false testimony. Unfortunately, that false witness was not around to assert a different claim. That held things up a bit.

Richard, on the other hand, had a far more pressing matter to attend to. He was locked in his hospital room, prescribed strict bed rest and medication to keep him above the water. He was approaching a critical point of survival, and every day counted. Jake walked in to see his dad struggling just to sit up enough to see the screen of the TV hanging in the corner. Jake moved over and gently lifted his dad from under his back.

"Hey, son," Richard said. Richard immediately doubled his efforts with his son at his side. "Okay, now pull!" He reached up. Jake braced him with his arm and tried to guide him. He didn't even feel heavy. It was Jake who was moving weights for someone else off the rack. Not even an exercise. Richard grunted and fell back. "Nah. Not going to happen...Okay, let go."

"Sure?" Jake asked. "One more time?"

Richard looked up, tired but motivated, and tried again, but it was no good.

"Nah, not going to happen," he admitted.

"Then I'll call the nurse?" Jake suggested. He lowered his dad down gently into the bed and sat beside him.

"No, it's fine," Richard said.

Jake took something out of his pocket. He didn't just come to try and play nurse for his dad. He retrieved the white-rock necklace and held it out. "This belongs to you," he said. "A white knight." He placed it in Richard's uncurled hand and smiled. Richard smiled back wistfully. A smile that was infinitely thankful but also full of regret.

They turned their attention to the TV. It piqued Jake's attention. He'd seen the people on the screen before. It was Callum, his last opponent, and another fighter from the same circuit. A comeback fight, an exhibition promotion before a main card. They were hyping it up as part of Callum's rise from the bottom after being broken in the ring. Then Jake saw his own fight, the overhead ringside view of Ragin' Jake giving the newcomer Callum a hideous beatdown until long after the bell had rung.

"Son," Richard uttered. Jake turned, expecting a horrified expression. Richard was fixed on the necklace in his hand. He looked upset.

"I'll call the nurse," Jake insisted.

"No," Richard whispered. His voice sounded dry.

"Thirsty?"

Richard looked up. His eyes were sunken. Jake could see his pain and his sadness. A body bereft of all his rage, and all his vengeance, with nothing to fill it out. That's what he saw in his aged old man. The only strength Richard had left was put into his hand as he curled his fingers around the memento.

"I think I'm ready," he said. "It's my time." Jake moved slightly to the right and looked over to the bedpan nearby. He turned to his dad for confirmation—desperately. Richard leaned his head back into his pillow. "I'm ready to go," he sighed. "Ready to die."

Everything went quiet. The TV kept playing, but Jake couldn't hear it. He couldn't take his eyes off of his father, but his father eventually lifted his eyes back up to the screen. Jake looked up. The program shifted to a commercial.

Jake cleared his throat, and the world returned to normal. He heard the sounds of medical machines and people in the hall and the TV buzzing and droning away about killer prices and outrageous deals.

"Now," Jake began, "I got to go...but I'll be back here tomorrow with chicken soup." He shot up to his feet, shaking with a slight, simmering fury. "And I'll be back the next day," he insisted, "and then the next day and then the next day after that." He pointed his finger assertively at Richard. "Us—our family—we aren't quitters. We're fighters." He turned and left in a huff. His rage wasn't all that drove him forward. There was fear, desperation, hopelessness—his rage tried its best to smother it all, but he was left seething with his teeth clenched.

As he went to leave, he ended up stopping in front of an open room that was hosting a man wounded many times over. Inside was a desperate-looking family who gathered around for what looked like a final moment. Even then, through the pain of it all, Jake saw the man try his hardest to smile and face his worried friends with strength. Jake slipped out with his hands in his pockets, gripping his legs.

He was back in town and back to square one. No longer a fighter, a top-billed crowd drawing spectacle maker. He was a killer, at least twice over. An indicter of life sentences for men with no lives to live but lives of destruction. He was the son of a killer and the brother of a fool, orphaned by the one person who made it all work together. He said much, but he felt like he was also at an end.

There was no one for him to beat up to feel better, no target for his fists to reach to draw a conclusion. He had nothing left in him but his rage and nowhere to put it. All he felt was heat and pain, too deep inside to flex or drain away....

Chapter 42

Six months went by. The criminal proceedings were all concluded. Tony and Harvey were charged posthumously for multiple counts of murder and a long list of gang conspiracies. The news wasn't major or day-breaking. It was just one more story of crime reaching further away than most would suspect. The cozy outer-city suburbs and inner-city strongholds only knew about the crime in the outback as a sort of fantasy to make it more dangerous. They'd never believed it unless it came for them next.

The civil trials were all but forgotten. Jake walked off his own separate charges from his street assault. It turned out the guy he hit was in much deeper legal trouble than anyone expected. Some of the drugs Tony's gang rolled out reached deep into the city, so all charges were unceremoniously dropped pending the other trial. Despite that, Jake apologized and agreed to attend AA meetings under the premise that it was the drinking that drove him to swing blindly.

Jake's deals all lapsed, and he was left with little money. It made sense for him to move somewhere low-cost and low-profile and keep it with someone he trusted that could help him tend the grounds. He settled into a nice little suburb where kids played freely in the streets on their days off from school. They were engaged in a light cricket game until a black car rolled through and chased them all out. Jake watched as the familiar-looking vehicle pulled up in front of his new home.

The house was a fixer-upper, something for a small family to work on and improve over the years, or for two young-ish and strong men to overhaul and repair over the course of a month in the sun. Jake stuck a shovel in the ground near where he and AJ dug a hole for a new awning extension and approached the car just as Brian exited and looked the place over.

"Hey Jake," he called out. As he arrived, Natasha exited the front door with two tall glasses of iced lemonade. She stood by and watched as the stranger approached Jake like an old friend. "One of the fighters told me I could find you here." He looked past Jake like he was a light post that couldn't be moved. "Neat place. Could we have a private chat for a moment?"

Jake looked over his shoulder to AJ, who looked ambivalent and eager to take a break. "Sure," he agreed. Brian put his hand on Jake's shoulder and guided him toward the house. AJ and Natasha watched as Jake—their Jake—got wrangled by a man much shorter and weaker looking. Natasha left the stairs just as they approached and went over to AJ's side.

"Who's that city slicker?" AJ asked.

She handed him a glass. "I don't know."

Brian took Jake just up to the porch, in the shade, and walked him over to the side furthest from the side of the yard where AJ stood. He was just shy of inviting himself right in when he saw through the front door and all the work that still needed to be done before it was a safe place for company.

"You'll be fighting a guy," Brian explained, "with a record of twelve zip. I'd say your biggest purse yet -."

"How much?" Jake asked.

Brian turned, excited to go on. "Pay-per-views, perks, sponsorship deals. That's only the beginning. An effort on your behalf, though. Possibly committing six months for the promotional side of things. You'd be traveling around the world."

It seemed like business as usual, what he was used to. He looked over at Natasha and AJ. Brian sensed his hesitation.

"The biggest payday yet," he insisted. "A fighter at your age must take advantage...." He caught a side-eye from Jake and made an apologetic eye-roll. "Pop into the office. We can have the contract signed by tonight?"

Jake rubbed his finger over his rough jaw and looked over at Natasha and AJ. He hesitated before speaking again and led off with a sigh, already dropping Brian's heart. "Listen, Brian, I ah...Ain't got it in me. But I can pay you back what I owe you."

"Money doesn't grow on trees, you know," an old but stubborn voice said. Jake turned and saw Richard hobble out with his cane in hand. He regained enough health in remission to properly walk around and had the mellow gait of a man with a heavy glaucoma prescription keeping him going.

"My old man," Jake said half-heartedly. "Hears, sees everything."

"Heard everything," Richard said. He pointed his cane at Jake. "Can't find any string at the back, maybe can't see so well." He walked over and readily held his hand out. "Hi. I'm Richard."

"Brian," Jake said, waving between them, "my dad, Richard."

Brian looked surprised by the strength in the old man's hand, and Richard looked satisfied. He looked up at his son and nudged him in the side. "So you going to take the offer or what? Seems foolish not to."

Jake looked over at Natasha and AJ again. He saw them looking up at him, pleased and encouraging. Natasha was happy, and AJ looked proud.

"Good old rage is gone, huh?" Brian said half-mockingly.

Jake looked in himself, down to the hollow place where his rage once dwelled. There really was nothing there. Inside himself, all he saw were the results of his rage. The bodies and the fires, bloody money, and Harvey's pulsing fountain of blood.

"I'm sorry -," Jake began.

"Just a moment," Richard interrupted. "Didn't you once say to me that this family isn't quitters; we are fighters?"

Jake was shocked to hear his own words come from his father's voice. Richard smiled, seeing that he'd reached past Jake's hollow self into something deeper.

Jake's eyes glimmered momentarily as he felt something else well up inside him, a denser and more profound feeling than his old rage. Something like pride and joy. But that wouldn't stand out on a proper billing card. He smiled and furrowed his brow. He had nothing left in his life to enrage him. But he would always be Raging Jake.

STEPHEN DEGENARO

Is an actor, screenwriter, producer…and lo and behold now an author.
Stephen has worked as an actor in feature films, TV series, theatre, short films and commercials. His credits can be viewed on IMDB.
He is a fan of mixed martial arts and the UFC combat sport.
Stephen lives in Melbourne, Australia with his fiancée.
Raging Jake is his first book.

COMING SOON

RAGING JAKE

THE MOVIE IN THE MAKING
www.ragingjakemovie.com